Bark from the tree exploded into flying bits…

The echo of a gunshot bounced between the canyon walls.

"Get down!" Marlee yelled. She shoved Hunter and her K-9 down as bullets whistled over their heads. They were open targets, unprotected. With each blast around them, she felt her body tense. Her gun arm trembled like never before. She was always a sure and steady shot.

What was going on with her?

Hunter sprawled low beside Marlee and the concern in his eyes told her he saw it, too. She wanted him to stop looking at her like that…like something was wrong with her.

The rapid beat of her pulse echoed through her head and she forced her breath to slow. She became aware of her erratic breathing.

"Marlee, talk to me," Hunter said, glancing around, bracing for the next shot. The sniper was still around.

Yet she couldn't respond…

Katy Lee is a *Publishers Weekly* bestselling author who writes character-driven romantic suspense that thrills and inspires readers. She's a multi-award nominee for the RITA® Award and the Daphne du Maurier Award. Katy lives in beautiful Utah and is a special education teacher. She runs a literary nonprofit called Story Haven Writers. Keep up with Katy and her latest news, including her monthly newsletter, *Novel Ideas*, at katyleebooks.com.

Books by Katy Lee

Love Inspired Suspense

Sunken Treasure
Permanent Vacancy
Amish Country Undercover
Amish Sanctuary
Holiday Suspect Pursuit
Cavern Cover-Up
Santa Fe Setup
Tracing a Kidnapper's Trail

Rocky Mountain K-9 Unit

Christmas K-9 Unit Heroes
"Silent Night Explosion"

Mountain Country K-9 Unit

Christmas K-9 Guardians
"Lethal Holiday Hideout"

Pacific Northwest K-9 Unit

K-9 National Park Defenders
"Yuletide Ransom"

Visit the Author Profile page at LoveInspired.com for more titles.

TRACING A KIDNAPPER'S TRAIL

KATY LEE

Recycling programs for this product may not exist in your area.

ISBN-13: 978-1-335-95757-3

Tracing a Kidnapper's Trail

This is a work of fiction. Names, characters, places and incidents are either the product of the author's imagination or are used fictitiously. Any resemblance to actual persons, living or dead, businesses, companies, events or locales is entirely coincidental.

For questions and comments about the quality of this book, please contact us at CustomerService@Harlequin.com.

® is a trademark of Harlequin Enterprises ULC.

Love Inspired
22 Adelaide St. West, 41st Floor
Toronto, Ontario M5H 4E3, Canada
www.LoveInspired.com

HarperCollins Publishers
Macken House, 39/40 Mayor Street Upper,
Dublin 1, D01 C9W8, Ireland
www.HarperCollins.com

Printed in Lithuania

Having forgiven you all trespasses; Blotting out
the handwriting of ordinances that was against us,
which was contrary to us, and took it out of the way,
nailing it to his cross.

—*Colossians* 2:13–14

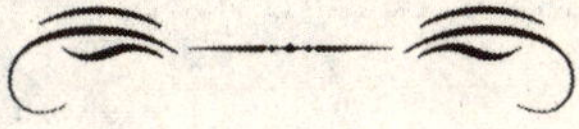

To Jack: You are a gift from God.

ONE

The metallic scent of blood carried on the Texas desert breeze, alerting the K-9 to a large amount of vital fluid spilled somewhere nearby. One whiff had Hunter Shelton's tawny search and rescue bloodhound, Libby, picking up her sleepy steps toward a slew of deputies from the Randall County Sheriff's Department. Typically, only coyotes and jackrabbits traipsed through Harmony Canyon State Park in the middle of the night—and the occasional hiker who didn't return from a trek through the eighty-mile-long and eight-hundred-foot-deep canyon. For Hunter, 2:00 a.m. phone calls typically meant someone had gone missing. Except this time, the body on the ground, lying facedown, with her long red hair knotted and splayed around her, wasn't in need of rescue any longer.

Perhaps if he had been called in sooner, the woman would have made it.

"Since when do I get called out for a crime scene? Not much Libby and I can do for her now." Hunter sidled up to Sheriff Steph Hawkins. "My days in law enforcement ended five years ago when I left the department. I'm search and rescue now. It's on the business card. West Texas Hill Country *Search and Rescue* Unit. I track living people. Remember?"

Sheriff Hawkins stood stoically and silent over the body.

His deputies were also thin-lipped while avoiding Hunter's gaze.

"What's going on?" The hair on the back of Hunter's neck stood at attention as he stretched for a closer look at the woman. "Who is it?"

The lanterns cast shadows all around her, and the excessive blood from her wounds made it hard to focus on her long enough to see beyond the heinousness of what someone had done to her. Sheriff Hawkins knelt to tilt her body and shone a flashlight onto her face.

Hunter's stomach twisted tighter and tighter then flipped. He thought he might be sick. The air in his lungs rushed out in one word. "Donna?"

"I'm sorry, Hunter," Sheriff Hawkins said, gently lowering Hunter's ex-fiancée back to the ground.

Hunter hadn't heard from her in nearly six years. They'd gone their separate ways. But that didn't make her murder meaningless to him. Or easier to handle.

"Couldn't you have told me over the phone? Prepared me, at least?"

The sheriff shook his head. "There's more. And it's the reason we called you out here."

Deputy Willis held up a child's backpack and a small sneaker with rainbows on it. "Your… Donna wasn't alone. There's evidence she had her daughter with her."

"Daughter?" That was news to Hunter. But he supposed a lot of time had passed—enough for her to find her true love and marry. Hunter tried to be happy for her, but that was hard to do when he was looking at her dead body. Her *murdered* body. "What was she doing out here? Have you called her husband? How long has she been here?"

Hawkins replied, "We estimate about six to eight hours. We pulled her info. She was living down in San Antonio and working at Channel 11 as a news anchor, but we don't see any record that she was married. Single parent of a five-year-old child, a little girl named Nancy Sue."

"Nancy Sue? That's the name we..." Hunter processed this information. He and Donna had once talked about the baby names they liked. Nancy Sue was a combination of their mothers' names. *It couldn't be.*

Nancy Sue couldn't be his...

The last night he'd seen Donna flashed in the forefront of his mind. One regretful night that had led to her walking out of his life forever. Shame had him dropping his gaze from the men he'd once worked with daily. He had been a different man then and so far from God.

Hunter swallowed hard, fighting to do the math. "Did you say the child is five?"

Sheriff Hawkins replied, "Yes. Birth date May 17. And yes, it adds up from when the two of you broke up. She really never told you about Nancy Sue?"

"Never. And there's no proof she's mine." Why was he defensive, all of a sudden? And over a woman he'd once loved?

The deputies shuffled a bit. Some dispersed to continue processing the scene. They would have a long night ahead of them, looking for trace evidence that would lead to Donna's killer and a missing or possibly abducted child. But Hunter realized they made themselves scarce to give him privacy while he accepted the same conclusion they'd already come to about his possible paternity.

Had he really fathered Donna's child? Talk about a gut punch.

But why would Donna keep that from me? Keep my child from me? He would have married her.

Except, Donna had been the one to call off the wedding. *She* had left *him*, returning the ring without even a goodbye.

After that night…

He looked down at her lifeless body and whispered, "I'm sorry." Even if he hadn't fathered her child, Hunter owed her an apology for letting that night go so far. Hunter had many people to apologize to for his behavior back then, but this was one apology he shouldn't have delayed on.

And now it was too late to make it up to her.

Or was it?

"Do you have any evidence of where the child went?" Hunter asked, knowing that he could find Donna's child and bring her to safety. His heart rate picked up, ready to find Nancy Sue. She could be out in this dark canyon alone. It mattered more to find her quickly. The clock had started eight hours ago…

Deputy Willis responded. "We found tracks that look like she ran from here, going north along the canyon wall. We didn't want to wait until daylight to set up a search. We figured you wouldn't, either."

"No. Call Gibbs. He'll gather our team. I'm starting now." Hunter's SAR Unit second-in-command, Michael Gibbs, would know what to do and have people out here within two hours. Hunter eyed the articles in Willis's hands. "Where did you find those? Right here? By her mother's body? That poor child saw her mother killed?"

The reality of the scene set in, unsettling his stomach more.

Deputy Willis said, "These tell us she was here. We don't know if she still is nearby or what she saw. Her mother could have told her to run. Or the child could have been caught and taken. We figured you and Libby could provide those answers."

Hunter took the pink backpack and rainbow shoe and bent to Libby, lifting the sneaker's interior toward the K-9's muzzle and famously sensitive nose. "Seek," he commanded, feeling panic rising in him like never before. Had a search and rescue ever been so personal? Even if Nancy Sue wasn't his child, she was the daughter of the woman he'd once planned to marry.

Hunter ignored the fact that he could search in this place for the rest of his life and barely cover a fraction of the expansive landscape. And the murder had happened as many as six or eight hours ago? That poor child. He felt minuscule—in size and power—compared to the looming, jagged red rock walls ensconcing him on either side and the nearly insurmountable undertaking he was embarking on.

He stood near the banks of a winding river that cut through the canyon's middle, shimmering in the moonlight before the dark of night obscured it for miles and miles in both directions, the river's only evidence the soft rushing sound of water that at any other time could soothe an anxious heart. Hunter pushed aside the fact that the river could also swallow a person whole forever. With Libby leading the way, he would know soon if that child was cloaked in the darkness nearby…or if someone or something had taken her.

"Please, Lord, guide me to this little girl."

Even after six years, Hunter considered himself a new believer, but he never planned to return to the man he once was. God knew everything about him and loved him still. Knowing this had allowed Hunter to begin his life over, a life devoted to his Redeemer. His past with women wasn't something he was proud of—it'd left him unwilling to open his heart to love since his breakup with Donna.

"Regardless of who fathered this child, she's Your precious little one. Use me to save her. Amen."

Libby sniffed the ground, zigzagging and snorting ferociously, eagerly, in all directions. Hunter felt the moment his K-9 latched on to the lead. The tug on the leash quickened

Hunter's steps. As much as he wanted Libby to track faster, to run ahead, his hurry could cause the dog to lose the scent.

Libby directed him toward the canyon wall, just where Sheriff Hawkins had believed the tracks led. Soon, away from the police light stands, Hunter found himself blinded by the night. He flipped the headlamp on his cap to illuminate his path as Libby rushed forward with her nose to the ground. Over rocks and even through thorned bushes, Libby didn't slow a step.

Hunter figured the child had to be ripped to shreds after traipsing through the large spiked lote bushes, especially missing a shoe. With every footfall, he prayed for her, but when Libby came to a stop and sat, Hunter saw no sign of a child.

"Hello? Sweetie, are you here?" He spoke low and calm, even though he wanted to shout. His headlight's beam bounced up and down and all the way around, exposing nothing but rocks and brush. A cluster of tumbleweeds against a large black mound caught his attention.

Leading Libby toward them, he stopped when he noticed the mounds were shiny. A closer inspection revealed they weren't rocks but black garbage bags, stuffed and bulging.

But with what?

Hunter turned at a crunch from behind him. He expected to see a deputy following him, but no one stood in the darkness. Shadows of trees and boulders cast against the canyon walls played tricks on his eyes, like growing and shrinking desert creatures that the breeze caused to move and dance.

"Willis? Sheriff?" Hunter called. "Do you know why these bags are here?"

No response.

Perhaps he had heard one of those rabbits springing about the desert floor. He hoped it was that and not a larger, more dangerous animal—or Donna's murderer still lurking. Hunter unhooked his holster just in case. He also removed his jackknife and flipped it up. In the next second, he carefully sliced open one bag, bracing for something heinous.

A used latex glove fell out...along with the stench of urine—*no,* ammonia. He split the bag wider and found a broken respirator. He knew what the articles were.

The bags were a meth dump. Used paraphernalia from a drug lab. A quick count down the line added up to twenty-six of them. These were from a huge drug operation.

And Nancy Sue's scent ended here.

Had the child run from one danger to another? Or were both scenes from the same danger? Hawkins had said Donna Hartman was a news anchor now, but he remembered when, as an investigative reporter, she would have done anything for the next big story. It was what broke them up when she crossed the line for a lead...and he nearly lost his job.

That she might've brought her daughter into danger for a story crossed a whole other line. A drug cartel leader, meth workers or a trafficking ring could have taken Nancy Sue. A child would bring a high price for them. His stomach threatened to retch again.

Hunter pocketed his knife for his phone. He needed to find the origin of these bags. Whoever dumped them could have Nancy Sue. He needed to find this meth lab...fast.

Pulling up the sheriff's number to alert him to the find, Hunter's thumb hovered over the call button.

He knew someone better to call in. One DEA agent with long, honey-blond hair who always got her drug lord, and probably without breaking a pink fingernail. Who sniffed out meth labs like Libby sniffed out her treat stash, no matter how great a hiding place Hunter thought he had found.

There was only one problem.

Agent Marlee Price hadn't spoken to him in eight years.

Not since the night she showed up at his apartment, and he had another girl there. Marlee's brother had just died from an overdose, and Hunter hadn't been there for her in her grief. She learned after that he was responsible for her brother's death…and she never spoke to him again.

Another apology he'd yet to make.

Hunter sighed and pulled up her number. A pair of green eyes flashed before him when a ten-year-old picture he'd taken appeared with her contact information. All he saw was the adoration on her face. For him. But those days ended the last time he laid eyes on her in person and let her down. She owed him nothing.

He made the call anyway.

Three rings. One more and the call would go to voicemail. He frowned but told himself he shouldn't be surprised she would reject his call. She could also be asleep or might not remember his phone number if she saw it on caller ID. Another crunch came from behind, and Hunter swung around to peer through the night. The ringing stopped, but silence followed.

"Marlee?" Hunter spoke to dead air on the phone while scoping the area around him. He moved to end the call as he stepped forward with Libby.

"You have a lot of nerve calling here, Shelton." Marlee's deep voice came through the phone, stopping Hunter in his tracks. He would know it anywhere. He grew up hearing his best friend's kid sister perpetually chase them—*"Wait up! Wait for me!"* Though it never bothered him as much as it did her brother, Ben.

"I know." Hunter closed his eyes and pushed forward. "And I know I don't deserve this, but I need your help. There's a missing child in Harmony Canyon. Her mother's been murdered, and it may all be connected to a meth lab. I wouldn't normally ask, but this one's hit close to home. Personal."

More silence. "Why me? I'm in Houston. There's a DEA office closer to you."

Another crunch from behind had Hunter swinging around again. His headlight illuminated a cactus. "You're right," he said absently, squinting into the dark. "I'm sor—"

Pain split Hunter's head as he fell to his knees, dropping the phone, Libby's leash and the pink backpack to the ground.

"Hunter? Are you there?" Marlee's voice could still be heard from the phone three feet away. But Hunter could only hold his head where he felt blood saturating his cap beneath his fingers.

Something had hit him. Or rather, *someone* had hit him.

He reached for his sidearm that he only carried for wildlife attacks. He doubted a rattler had done this to him. Fighting the urge to close his eyes, he worried he would miss his shot, anyway. His vision doubled as he saw two of Libby running off into the darkness. A shuffling sound to his left caused him to brace for another strike.

"Hunter?" Marlee shouted, but her voice sounded fainter than before. "Answer me! If this is some kind of joke, I'm not laughing!"

He opened his mouth to speak, but he was pretty sure he was only thinking the words. He groaned and spoke over the splitting pain. "Call Sheriff… Hawkins."

He lifted his head to light the surrounding area, realizing that not only was his dog gone, but so were the pink backpack and shoe, the only connections he had to Nancy Sue's scent.

Marlee ended the call with Sheriff Hawkins, who assured her they would find Hunter. Still, she grew frustrated with not knowing and nearly called Hunter back. But perhaps the best thing to do was to show up and see him for herself. If she left now, she'd be there in four hours, right around sunrise.

But why should she jump at his call?

Hunter Shelton was from her past and better off left there. But he also had been in distress. This case was more than a missing child, just as he'd said.

Personal.

Someone had been murdered. Someone he knew. There were also drugs involved, and that was her specialty.

Marlee felt the typical excitement for the hunt well up within her. She and Gustav sniffed out drug houses daily for the pure joy of it. She'd vowed to shut down every one of the despicable sites.

For Ben.

But Ben would expect her to help his lifelong best friend now. Could she do this for her brother? Could she face the man she blamed for Ben's death? She hadn't spoken to Hunter in eight years and had never planned to again.

Except, here she was climbing out of bed, knowing in a few hours, their paths would cross regardless.

For Ben and for a missing child, she told herself as she pulled down her packed suitcase from the top shelf of her closet, always ready to travel at a moment's notice. By the moonlight peeking over the treetops at her apartment complex, Marlee made a second call. This one to her boss.

It also went to voicemail.

"SAC Williams, I need to head out of town for a consult on a drug and missing-persons case." She brushed her teeth as she left the message for him. She thought it odd he didn't pick up. He always answered, no matter the time, day or night.

Maybe he was exhausted. Her team, along with her K-9, had taken down Clint Jackson's biggest meth lab in Houston last week. After two years of methodical planning and investigating, they took it by SWAT. Gustav should earn a medal for his expert narcotics skills. SAC Williams, too, for his constant trust in her abilities.

Marlee dressed quickly and scooped her long blond hair into a ponytail. The heat would rise soon enough in West Texas, even for March. She hit the lights and grabbed her car keys off her nightstand, along with her Sig, securing it at her belt's holster. At the bedroom door next to hers, she swung it wide.

"Hey, buddy. You want to go play?"

The velvety black-and-tan German shepherd narcotics K-9 stood at attention, waiting for her next direction. His black eyes twinkled in delighted alertness. She grabbed the duffel bag she always kept at the ready, attached Gustav's leash to his tan bulletproof vest and led him from the town house. On the porch, she stopped cold.

Her parked SUV typically glowed in the beam of the lantern pole behind it.

Typically.

A quick analysis proved the lantern had been smashed. She took slow steps as she approached her vehicle, eyeing for any shadows beneath it and circling for a view of the passenger side.

"Guard," she commanded Gustav as she released his leash to remove her weapon and phone. Turning the flashlight on, she approached the rear of the vehicle to peer inside. A push of the hatch button lifted the door to Gustav's oversize crate. She moved to the back door on the driver's side and opened it, dropping the duffel on the seat. As if nothing was wrong, she pulled the driver's door wide and crouched low—just as gunfire exploded in the crisp air. The door took the hit, acting now as her shield.

"Get in the car!" she ordered Gustav. He obeyed instantly,

but his rippling energy and wagging tail showed he wanted to hunt down the shooter.

Her phone buzzed in her hand, and the caller ID showed SAC Williams returning her call. She hit the green circle with her thumb while she held her Sig in the other hand.

"Perfect timing," she said. "I'm being shot at."

"Already? I thought I would have a few minutes."

"Few minutes for what?" Another bullet hit the door. "Can you get me some backup, please? I'm at my apartment."

"You need to get out of there. Right now, Price. Jackson put a hit out on you and Gustav."

Marlee chuckled. "We really got under his skin with that drug bust, didn't we?"

"And every dealer and maybe even user will attempt to collect the bounty. Can you move out?"

"Gustav's in the car, so yes. I think I can make a getaway."

"Good. I have men on the way. Now, move out."

Marlee grumbled about leaving the scene and the shooter free, but she also knew she had no provisions for a standoff. Sliding into the SUV, she stayed low and started the engine, putting it into gear immediately and flooring the pedal for the exit.

"Get down. On the floor!" she ordered Gustav.

Bullets smacked the side of her vehicle, jolting her, but she kept moving…until she couldn't go any farther. Another truck was moving in from a side street in to block her path, but that wasn't happening. She floored it, sailing past the SUV to her right.

She caught the sight of Clint Jackson smirking over the steering wheel, his black hair covering one eye, as he aimed an assault rifle at her.

Marlee had just enough time to crouch as bullets shattered her passenger window and blistered the driver's seat where her head had just been. Bits of cushion flew into the air. If she had been a split second too late… The sight and noise stunned her like never before. Cowering low and covering her head, she managed to keep the car straight as she sailed down the street, making her escape. If she still prayed, she would have called out to God. But when the words were on her lips, she sealed them tight.

Tires squealing filled the early morning, followed by silence. She was glad no other drivers were out at this hour. She heard the wail of sirens and saw the oncoming flashing of red and blue lights. Cop cars crowded in from behind, too, from what she caught in her rearview, before Marlee pressed on.

She'd have to pull over before she left and check the damage to her SUV, but for the moment, she was putting as much distance between her and Clint Jackson as possible.

Hunter's call for help couldn't have come at a better time—she needed to get out of town, and fast.

TWO

"Gustav, sit," Marlee commanded her dog at the end of the leash as she scanned the faces of the SAR team before her. They'd all gathered in the canyon at the closest ranger station to where the body had been found. Marlee halted on the one who had called her west in the middle of the night—the man she thought she would never see again…the one she'd once, in her youthful naivete, dreamed she would marry someday. But then he'd killed her brother.

Hunter Shelton wore a cap over his blond curls, but a few peeked out, along with evidence of a bandage wrapped around his head.

So, he had been injured.

A surge of protectiveness reared its head within her. She squashed it immediately, having no reason to feel such a thing for this man.

She approached him. "What happened?" she asked, trying to ignore the way her heart rate picked up in an instant at the sight of him.

Another feeling that needed to be sent packing.

"A rock hit my head."

"I hate when that happens." Marlee tried to be snarky about his lack of details, but her voice cracked with sudden dryness. Somehow, she knew her reaction at seeing Hunter would have been the same, even if he hadn't been hurt. She should turn back and hightail it out of there right away. SAC Williams had met up with her before she'd left Houston and offered her his SUV. She was glad not to have to drive around in a bullet-ridden vehicle. Though, facing the end of Clint Jackson's gun again would be safer for her than admitting that Hunter and his fierce hazel eyes still caused her heart to yearn to care for him—and whatever else it wanted to do. Why did she think she could treat this like any other case? Not even cutting ties with the man eight years ago had changed her reactions to him.

"This was a bad idea," she mumbled. Just as bad as the night she showed up at his apartment to tell him she loved him after Ben's death. She had just learned how fragile life was, and didn't want to wait another second before confessing her feelings.

Terrible idea.

"We needed you," Hunter replied, stepping forward. "I never thought you would show up, but thank you. This is my team." He looked at the man next to him. "You remember Michael Gibbs? We played football together in college. He's my partner now."

Marlee vaguely remembered the guy but nodded as though she did.

"Marlee Price is a Texas hero." Hunter told his partner, then faced her again. "I read about the meth lab you took down last week, tucked in a neighborhood in Houston. You caught it right before it could have blown the house and the surrounding homes into bits. You saved a lot of lives, Marlee. I'm really proud of you."

She shrugged, not up to receiving anything from this man, especially accolades. And actually surprised he would be impressed with her work, knowing he bought the drugs that killed her brother. But she needed to focus on the case at hand, not one that had no closure for her. "I'm already here. No need to lay on the praises. Just tell me about the case."

Hunter nodded, straightening to his full six feet. He reached for a photo in Michael's hand. It was of a little girl with big, brown curls. She was missing her two front teeth and had intense hazel eyes like Hunter's. Was it something in the water out here?

"Nancy Sue Hartman," Hunter stated, as though he was briefing a room around a conference table. "This is her kindergarten photo taken two months ago. We believe if we find a certain meth lab, we'll find her."

Marlee studied the picture for so long, the men showed signs of discomfort, shifting their feet and rubbing the backs of their necks. She needed to say something, but no words formed on her lips. This child looked just like Hunter, sans the blond hair for Nancy Sue's brown.

Personal, he had said. But just how personal?

Suddenly, her dog whined, ready to work. Hunter's red bloodhound did the same, but thankfully, both animals stayed by their handlers' sides.

Marlee lifted her gaze to the group, pressing her lips into a frown. "I don't find people. I hunt down drug houses. You mentioned a meth lab. I'll start there. The sheriff can handle the…" She looked straight at Hunter. "Missing child. And just so everyone here knows, I typically run my own investigations and I'm not up for changing my methods. So, if it's all right with you all, *I* will be in charge of the drug operation case. In other words, I don't work well with others."

A man in a tan uniform, with a badge that said he was park director Elliott Graham, puffed his burly chest. His reddened face barely controlled his disdain. "This is *my* park, and *I* am in charge. Of everything that goes on here. Nothing happens without my consent. We don't need federal agents on state property. If I had my way—"

"Then have it your way." Marlee shrugged and turned for the SUV, walking out of Hunter's life as fast as the last time. She'd never looked back on that horrid night and didn't plan to this time.

"Marlee, wait," Hunter called to her from behind. He reached for her arm, causing her to flinch at his touch. She stopped, but her pulse picked its pace where his hand had covered her wrist.

"I'm sorry," he said, releasing her quickly. His bright hazel eyes flashed bluer, reflecting the blue chambray shirt he wore. She wouldn't let him make her feel guilty for not wanting him near her, even if her heart rate said otherwise. He was the only one who had guilt to live with. As far as she was concerned, he had blood on his hands. Not her.

"Please don't let Elliott keep you from doing what you do best." Hunter leaned in, speaking low. His eyes pleaded for her to stay. Small blond curls brushed the nape of his neck, so inviting. She itched to loop them around her fingertips like she had once before, so many years ago. When she was young and naive.

Marlee blinked the memory away, needing to regroup. She didn't let on that her hasty retreat from him had more to do with the surprising flutters in her chest than some park ranger refusing her demands. She couldn't remember the last time she'd felt such an unsettling feeling—even more disturbing than the target on her back in Houston.

She'd had no idea being here would bring back long-dormant, heady feelings she used to experience around him over eight years ago. Back when she was too immature to recognize they were unwarranted and stemmed from a youthful infatuation, pure and simple. Back when she didn't know about who he really was…and his untrustworthiness. But she knew everything now, and even if her heart had forgotten the truth about her childhood crush, her mind hadn't. Hunter was bad news. Besides, he was a married man now.

Or so she had heard.

A glance at his empty left hand had her second-guessing that rumor. Maybe he didn't wear a ring on the job.

Marlee shrugged the inconsequential questions aside and lifted her chin, meeting Hunter's imploring gaze. She reminded herself of how he had let her brother down. Benny would still be alive if it hadn't been for this man. Slowly, the truth sent the flutters in her chest fleeing across the Texas desert with the rolling tumbleweeds. She filled her lungs with enough air to speak evenly.

"Why would you ever call me?" she whispered.

Hunter shrugged with his palms up. "You were the first person who came to my mind. Perhaps because you're the closest thing to Ben, and I needed my friend."

She shook her head. Ben was off the table for discussion. "You said this was personal. How so?"

Hunter looked at the picture in his hand. "This child is… Well, never mind. They're all important to me. I'm stumped, Marlee. All I know is time is short and I'm wasting every second standing here. You know how much I hate wasting time."

Marlee felt her lips cracking into a smile as she recalled that about him, but she quickly recovered her seriousness. Wasting time had always been his pet peeve. She could still hear his truck horn blaring from the front yard when he came to pick up Ben for football practice. Marlee would run to her bedroom window, always hoping for a glimpse of Hunter.

"Tell your brother to hurry up!" he would holler up to her, and she would do his bidding.

But not anymore.

Except, here she was, halfway across the state of Texas because he'd called her. She also sensed he hadn't been completely honest with her about the missing child. She'd have to fish the truth out of him soon, but she wasn't about to turn away from the search at this point. Marlee straightened her shoulders. "This is nothing but a case, got it?"

"We'll play it however you want."

More search team members filtered out from canyon trails. They made their way to Hunter and the park director, but before Elliott could give them a command, Marlee looked for Hunter to set the stage.

"Elliott, I know this is your park, but Marlee is running the drug investigation. The meth lab and…" Hunter looked to her for a nod. "And wherever that leads her. I trust her, and you can too."

Elliott Graham was double her size, but she was glad to see he didn't throw his weight around again. With a nod, he headed to his car to buddy up with a woman ranger.

"Ranger Charlie Woodridge, ma'am," the woman said as she passed. "We sure appreciate your help in finding this little one." The woman introduced herself with a nod before climbing into Graham's passenger seat. "I'm sure Hunter especially does."

Marlee wondered again about the connection Hunter had with the child.

Michael said to Hunter, "May I join the search team? If you're all set here and don't need me for anything at the scene, I'd like to keep looking." The man avoided her gaze as he waited for Hunter to respond.

"Go ahead, Michael. I think the agent and I can search the scene where Donna… Where the body was found and the scene of the meth dump." Hunter passed Michael the keys. "Take the truck. I'll drive with Marlee. The rest of the team is searching at mid-park by Red Ledge Trail next. Head on over there."

"Got it, boss." Michael turned to move out but cast an odd glance her way. The look lasted less than a second, but long enough for Marlee to catch a bit of disdain for her. Though she supposed she hadn't been the warmest person in the bunch. She needed to remember she had no beef with these people, except maybe to question their friendship with Hunter.

With Hunter's bloodhound loaded up in the back with her German shepherd, Marlee settled behind the driver's wheel again. Once Hunter buckled up, she fixed her gaze on the curving ribbon of asphalt that flowed into the deep, narrow Harmony Canyon.

"The crime scene is about a fifteen-minute ride from here," Hunter stated, cutting into the quiet broken by only a few whines from the dogs in the back.

Marlee drove in silence, gripping the wheel with white knuckles. She needed to set the stage with him, too. This was not a conversation she wanted to have, but it had to be done if they were going to work with each other. "I'm only here for the case. We talk about nothing else but the case. Understand?"

"Of course. But—"

"No buts. How was the mother murdered?"

Hunter sighed but answered, "Stabbed."

"How many times?"

"Fifteen."

"He knew her. And I'm not saying the killer is male. It could have very well been her best friend. But just for the sake of discussion, I'm saying he. Fifteen stab wounds tell me this was personal."

"It definitely looked…revengeful."

Marlee glanced his way to see him close his eyes. Why the man had ever become a cop was beyond her. He had always been too empathetic. Going into search and rescue fit him so much better than chasing down bad guys. She nearly asked him why and when he'd made the switch but bit her tongue, keeping to her demand that they only talk about the case.

As her gaze moved back to the view ahead of her, she caught sight of his empty ring finger again. Had she heard wrong about him being married?

"Tell me about her." Marlee cleared her throat. "The victim, I mean. What did she do for a living?"

"Journalist. She won an award last year for a story. She was a go-getter, that's for sure. Landed a news anchor position in San Antonio."

"A pretty far distance to come for a walk in the park in the middle of the night. She could have been lured out here, far away from her support system. Success sometimes means you step on some people on the way up the ladder. Maybe one of them wanted their sweet revenge."

Hunter raised his eyebrows. "You think her death may have been a corporate ego battle gone too far?"

Marlee shrugged. "I track drug pushers. What do I know of premeditated murder?" She felt her chest tighten and added, "But if *I* should end up dead, the trail stops at Clint Jackson." She exhaled a deep breath to push through the strange feeling building up inside. Maybe a little indigestion.

Hunter shifted to face her. His eyes now demanding. "What are you talking about? Who's Clint Jackson? And why does he want to kill you?"

She cleared her throat and took another deep breath. "Drug lord. And it's nothing big to worry about. After last week's bust, Jackson's coming for Gustav."

"And you?"

"Sure."

"Sure?" Hunter's voice rose. "Just how serious is this?"

She'd said too much. "I would rather talk about this case."

"If you're in danger, then it affects this case. How serious is he?"

"Jackson has no idea where I am. Only my boss, SAC Williams, knows."

"I assume Jackson has an army everywhere. It won't take him long to get your 411. What's he offering for you?"

Marlee pressed her lips, thinking of what SAC Williams had told her earlier that morning before she drove out. Before Hunter commanded an answer like an order to his K-9, she replied, "A hundred grand for Gustav."

"And?"

She mumbled, "Twenty for me. He wants Gustav dead more. Or maybe Jackson plans to use him to sniff out his competitors. Regardless, I won't let him near my dog."

Hunter huffed a bitter laugh. "So nonchalant. Marlee, you're a walking target. Please tell me you understand that."

Marlee thought of the shootout at her apartment. The image of her bullet-ridden SUV dried her throat. Her chest tightened again.

Yeah, she understood she had a bull's-eye on her back.

In the next second, a loud pop filled the SUV, and the steering wheel jerked right. Marlee gripped tight as the vehicle careened off the pavement, a large rock wall coming straight at them. Someone was trying to kill her…again.

Hunter noticed Marlee's reaction slowed to the point the vehicle was heading straight for the red canyon wall, and she'd yet to turn the wheel. Quickly, he reached over and yanked the steering wheel to the right, fishtailing the back end and spinning the SUV around. They careened violently in a spray of gravel and cacti until they came to an abrupt stop mere feet from the solid wall that could have killed them. Why hadn't she turned the wheel? One look at her ashen face had him zipping his lips. Something was going on with her, and he doubted she would share.

Instead, he focused on what had caused the blowout…or what had sounded more like a gunshot. Had the sound scared her? A glance around the area needed to be his priority, just in case someone was out there taking shots at them. He had seen a flash in the shrubs at the same moment as the pop.

The flash of a gun?

Or just a glint of sunlight?

Hunter didn't want to jump to conclusions, but Marlee had just told him she and Gustav had rewards out for their heads. Someone had also knocked him on the head with a rock last night and taken Nancy Sue's backpack and sneaker. Of course, with his injury, he might be seeing flashes.

Still, he wasn't about to let Ben's kid sister out of the vehicle just yet, even if she was a federal agent. A quick glance in the rearview told him the dogs appeared fine.

"Stay low." He removed his Glock.

"For a flat tire?" She seemed more like herself again as the color came back to her cheeks. She pushed open the driver's door and stepped out.

"I saw something." He pulled her back inside and opened his door with his gun held in front of him. Using the roof of the SUV as a shield, he slunk to the end to look toward the shrubbery where he had seen the glint. From this angle, he didn't notice any movement.

"What'd you see?" she asked from behind him.

He looked to his right and found Marlee coming up beside him with her gun drawn.

The desert wind flickered the shrub branches, but that was all the movement he noticed. "Maybe I imagined it, but I thought I saw the flash of a gun going off. Next thing I knew, we were heading for the wall."

Marlee scanned the area, then with a shake of her head, she holstered her gun and opened the hatch to check on the dogs.

"They're both fine," she called to him. "Nothing out here but lizards and rocks."

"I'll check the tire." Hunter made his way around to the driver's side and knelt to inspect the front wheel. Feeling with his fingertips, he examined the surface but found it too shredded to make a judgment call. "You have a spare?"

Marlee was already holding it in her hand along with the jack. "One step ahead of you. You want to do the honors?"

Hunter reached for the jack. "Guard my back." When she didn't move, he continued, "You can go back to hating me after I've changed your tire."

"I can change it myself."

"I know. I taught you how. But right now, I want you to be alert. I already lost one… I mean, I already have one dead body. I don't need another." Hunter reasoned his response stemmed from a need to protect his old best friend's sister, but the idea of Marlee ending up like Donna choked him. She had always been special to him, and even with the years between them, she still was. Maybe he should let her change the tire so he could stand guard over her.

Marlee squinted down at him. "Who'd you lose?"

Hunter knew his slipup had created a host of questions he couldn't answer until he had answers himself. He continued before she asked more questions about Donna and before he said something he couldn't retract, "I lost a lot. And that's all I'm going to say about that. Besides, didn't you just tell me there's a price on your head?"

Thankfully, Marlee turned away, holding her gun high, and kept watch, forfeiting the battle. But for how long? At some point, there would be a hill between them she would be willing to die on. Her hatred for him ran deep. His guilt ran deeper. He knew she would hold him accountable someday. Maybe then he would have the peace that eluded him for so long.

Hunter cranked the jack, lifting the SUV high enough to swap out one tire for the other. He rolled the shredded wheel to the back and hefted it inside.

Libby let out a soft huff, and Hunter patted both dogs to reassure them. He reached into his denim pockets to remove two small treat bones. Both dogs caught theirs in their mouths and retreated to the back of the crate to enjoy.

"Any sign of a shooter?" Hunter asked after closing the hatch. He searched the surrounding canyon, and all was quiet. It was safe to say the tire had been just a blowout from a sharp rock. He kicked some beneath his boots, noticing there were many that could do damage.

Hunter realized Marlee hadn't answered his question. "Are you ready to go?"

Marlee still didn't respond. She stood with her gun straight out and her legs locked. Did she see something he missed?

He stepped up beside her, but instead of following her gaze, he looked at her profile. A sheen of sweat glistened on her upper lip. He touched her forearm, and she flinched.

She glared at him. "I thought you wanted me to stand guard," she said in irritation.

"It's time to go. Are you all right?" Hunter studied her rapid eye movement.

"Oh. Right. Yeah, I'm fine." She brought the gun to her holster, but not before he noticed a tremor in her hands.

Falling in behind her, he asked, "Do you want me to drive?"

He expected her to balk, but she made her way to the passenger side without a word. Hunter refrained from asking if she was okay again. She wouldn't tell him, anyway. After a few moments of driving, she jumped back into the case.

"Tell me about the meth connection."

He followed her lead to change the subject. "Twenty-six black trash bags filled with toxic chemical waste were found not too far from the body, with evidence Nancy Sue had been at the dump site."

"What paraphernalia was in the bags?"

"Glassware, antifreeze containers and other materials like that. Some contaminated sheets, clothing, shoes, gloves and respirators were also in there. Something interesting about the items were the Canadian labels on the chemical canisters."

She nodded. "We see that a lot. Drug labs are increasingly using chemicals from Canada, where they can be obtained more easily. I would say at almost thirty trash bags, you were probably looking at about forty-five pounds of meth. I'll give Gustav the clothes and gloves to see if he can pick up a scent."

"Most of the items from Nancy Sue's home were taken to the Sheriff's department. But I kept a few personal items for tracking in the field. Just in case."

"In case of what?" She tucked her long, shimmery, honey-blond hair behind her ear, giving him a better view of her flawless skin. The morning sun glowed on her face in a fiery light. She wore canvas cargo pants, hiking boots and a long-sleeved pale blue shirt, open at the throat to reveal a white tank top trimmed with lace.

It was 100 percent Marlee Price.

Even back in her college years, she commanded attention but never lost her sweet edge. Now, she was taking down the meanest of bad guys with that .40-caliber Sig Sauer on her hip holster, reminding everyone not to let the smile fool them. He'd made that mistake once.

He had taken Marlee for granted back in the days when she

followed him around like a shadow, believing she would always be a part of his life. And he would be a part of her family. His dose of reality came swiftly eight years ago when he forgot that family came with responsibility.

He failed that test.

But now, here she was sitting with him, helping him solve a case. Did he dare hope to make amends?

No.

But he would thank God for the opportunity to try.

"In case you showed up," he answered her question with honesty. He'd learned with Marlee that was the only way. "I wasn't sure if you would. I definitely don't deserve it, but… I'm glad you're here."

She shrugged nonchalantly. "I didn't have much choice."

Again, he thought of the hit put out on her, and he felt sick to his stomach. All Hunter wanted to do was barricade her in a safe house…where she belonged. Instead, he pasted on a smile. "I can't say I'm glad for the reason, but you made a smart choice getting out of Houston. But then, you always were smarter than I gave you credit for. A mistake I won't make again."

The boulder that Donna's body had been found behind appeared on the horizon. The scorching sun shimmered over the pavement, giving the landscape a smoldering illusion. He pulled the car over and pointed at the rock. Police tape whipped in the wind with pieces already broken since the early morning.

"You want to see where the body was found? Or go right to the meth dump site?"

"Since we're here, let's take a look." Marlee opened her door and began the trek up an incline. At the police line, she stopped and surveyed the land with her hands on her hips.

She glanced up at the sun and down at her feet before circling around.

"Did she have a car? Or did she hike out here?" Marlee asked.

"We found no sign of a vehicle."

"Where's the closest campground?"

Hunter smiled. "Are you sure homicide isn't your gig? Already checked. No car there, either."

"There's no way she hiked in here with a five-year-old. Someone dropped her off. Or brought her out here. Are you sure she wasn't killed somewhere else and dumped here?"

"The crime scene investigator didn't think so. My only concern is finding the child. I just took his word for it about the murder."

She brushed past him to return to the truck. "And my only concern is finding the drug lab. Something tells me this Donna Hartman got herself into some trouble."

Hunter mumbled under his breath. "It wouldn't have been the first time."

THREE

The dump site had been cleared of the trash bags, but Marlee was more concerned with why the meth lab workers chose this area to discard their waste. The trail to the site wasn't blatantly on the roadside, but it also wasn't hidden from the public eye. A person would have to walk around two jagged rocks and various-size trees to join the trail, but the drug workers still could have chosen a more isolated spot.

"They wanted the waste to be found quickly," she said, with Gustav sniffing the ground by her side. She turned to see Hunter and Libby focused on a shrub. "Is she tracking something?"

Hunter lifted his gaze to the surrounding cliffs, breathing deeply. The way he snapped to made it look like he had been in a daze. Something was on his mind that he wasn't sharing.

"What's going on with you?" she asked.

He hesitated for a few seconds, then said, "There's more to this search and rescue than is typical. I keep thinking of what Nancy Sue might have witnessed. And I keep thinking of the flash of light at the blowout. It all has me on edge, I guess."

Marlee nodded, appreciating Hunter's reminder that a little girl's life was at stake, but also her mental state. Marlee released some of her drive to track a drug house and thought of the danger that little girl was in—and them by being out here tracking her.

"It was probably the sun." She looked behind her. "But it'd be wise to stay alert."

He nodded to her holster. "We'll just be careful. It's smart to carry your Sig."

"Wouldn't leave home without it." She patted her sidearm. "Though Gustav is a better protector than any bullet."

Hunter smiled at Gustav, then Libby. "Protector and tracker. We got ourselves a great team."

Marlee didn't fully agree with him calling them a team, but kept her thoughts to herself. "We're going to catch these bad guys and find that little girl. I think if we focus on our goals and trust our dogs to lead the way, we can't go wrong."

Hunter smiled, but the joy didn't reach his eyes. "You always went after what you wanted. Your record of successful takedowns proves you're not to be messed with. But knowing people are coming after you has me afraid for you."

Before Marlee could tell him not to be, he cut her off and continued, "You're Ben's little sister. Don't tell me not to worry about your safety. There are days I still think of you as my own."

"As your sister?" The comment shouldn't have bothered Marlee. When she was younger, it probably would've sent her into a complete tantrum. Never did she think of Hunter as a brother. But now she didn't want to think of him at all. So, why did it matter how he viewed her, then *or* now?

Hunter continued, "He would want me to do whatever possible to keep you safe from these people coming after you. He hated letting you down when you needed him the most."

Marlee held her tongue about how Hunter had let her down more than Ben ever did. Ben had had a problem, but he would still be alive if Hunter had acted as a true friend. "Just do me a favor," she said. "Don't hide anything from me. If you see anything suspicious, tell me. I don't need your protection. I only want the truth."

"Even if the truth will kill you?" Suddenly, she knew they weren't talking about the bounty hunters coming for her. They weren't talking about finding this meth lab or even the little girl.

But kill me? That seemed a little over the top. Why would Hunter think Ben's drug problem would've killed her?

Because I idolized him.

The answer came swiftly. Remembering the anguish of not being able to save him sent her spiraling, but if she had known before his death, she would've given up everything to help him end his addiction.

Even if it killed her.

"I still want the truth," she said. "I'm not a little girl anymore. I'm a federal agent. And I won't rest until I shut down as many of these empires as I can."

"Rest is a gift from God." Hunter moved away from her, leading Libby toward a shallow depression in the terrain. "We're not meant to do it all. You're not meant to catch every bad guy and take down every meth house. It's impossible to take on the world. That's God's job."

She glanced at him quickly. "When did you become so… spiritual?"

"Six years ago. I hit my lowest point and God picked me up. Maybe I'll tell you about it sometime."

"No, thanks." Marlee had no desire to talk about God. After Ben's death, she had turned her back on Him. She had once trusted Him completely, and He had played a cruel joke on her. She had read her Bible and believed every word, including all the places that said God was supposed to protect them.

"God may have picked you up, but He failed me," she said. "Now I take matters into my own hands. Hand me the item you kept from the trash bags and let's get this search started."

Hunter paused for a second, looking like he wanted to negate her words. Thankfully, he kept his mouth shut and reached into his coat pocket. Removing a clear plastic evidence bag with a blue latex glove inside, he took a step toward her to hand it over.

"This was in one of the meth bags. Hopefully Gustav catches a scent," he said. "One of the officers' K-9s wasn't able—"

Bark from the tree beside them exploded into flying bits, and Hunter grabbed for her. The echo of the gunshot bounced between the canyon walls.

Marlee yelled, "Get down!" She shoved him down over Libby while she covered Gustav from the bullets whistling over their heads. She withdrew her weapon, but with no idea where the shooter was hiding, they were open targets, unprotected. With each blast around them, she felt her body tense and soon freeze, even while her heart rate sped up. Her breathing shortened and wheezed in her ears. She watched her extended arm with her gun tremble like never before. She was always a sure and steady shot.

What was going on with her?

Hunter sprawled low beside her and the concern in his eyes told her he saw her reaction, too. She wanted him to stop looking at her like that…like something was wrong with her.

Finally, the gunshots stopped, but she still couldn't move. In the silence that followed, the rapid beat of her pulse echoed through her head so loud that she figured Hunter could hear it. She forced her breath to slow and her ears to listen for any sounds from the shooter. Beside her, Hunter remained still.

She became aware of her erratic breathing, thankful that she was breathing and not hurt.

"Marlee, talk to me." Hunter didn't move a muscle. The sniper was still around.

No response formed on her lips.

He moved a fraction of an inch, shifting closer to her side, acting as her shield, as she had done for him after the first shot. He moved another inch closer and soon he was able to look directly at her face. Hunter shifted her into a crevice on the ground, hiding her and Gustav a bit more in the hole.

"You were right. It was the flash of a gun on the road," Marlee whispered.

"Do you always react this way to gunfire?"

Marlee couldn't answer. Nausea pushed bile up into her throat. Tamping it down, she said, "No. It must be the heat." Her excuse sounded ridiculous…and weak. "Or maybe anxiety, I guess. I've had a lot going on today. Things out of the ordinary. Present company included."

"Sorry to cause you anxiety." Hunter glanced down into her eyes, studying her intensely. The concern on his face said she must not look well. She knew she didn't feel well. Whatever was happening to her had never happened before. But what was it? She turned her face away to avoid his scrutinizing.

Scanning the area, she focused on the threat. "All I can see is grass and dirt and the trunk of a Piñon tree. There are red rocks surrounding us, but we're still too exposed to stand or move from the spot. I don't see any sign of the shooter."

"The man must be camouflaged. Maybe he's wearing a sand-colored ghillie suit. Possibly ex-military."

"Ex-military turned meth lab operator?" She rolled her eyes. "I suppose it's possible."

"Sad if so. I've seen some crazy things before. Camouflage suits that matched the terrain wouldn't be something that could be purchased at the sports store in town. But whoever the shooter is, he could have stolen it from the military or made his own."

"Drug operations don't spare any expense for protecting their businesses."

"Apparently, if they're willing to pay out a hundred and

twenty grand for DEA agents and their K-9s." Sarcasm dripped thickly in his voice.

"Can we not talk about that right now?"

Hunter huffed. "Sure. The shooter has precision. Perhaps a trained sniper, which also says ex-military."

"Except, he missed." Marlee tried to laugh, but her voice hitched.

He lifted his head a little higher above her. Instantly, another blast of gunfire spat dirt in front of them. Marlee jumped, jolting against Hunter.

"Hey, it's okay," he whispered.

"You're lying."

"Yes. We aren't out of the woods yet. One wrong move and we're dead. We need to get out of here somehow. But I don't dare move you."

"Because you think my legs won't hold me up?"

"Hey, you said it."

Another round came their way, this time to their left. The sounds brought on another wave of panic. Marlee clenched her teeth to control her wheezing.

"He's on the move," Hunter said. "His position is changing. Might be farther away now. I'm going to call for help." Slowly, Hunter reached for the radio at his waist. He winced a little as he moved to bring the radio to his lips, and she vaguely wondered why.

"Ranger, do you copy?" he said low.

"This is Ranger One. Copy." Elliott's voice came through the speaker.

"We need help. A sniper is shooting at us at the drop site. How far out are you?"

"We'll be right there."

"He might be camouflaged. Be careful."

"Roger that. Over."

Hunter laid the radio beside them. "Hang in there. It won't be long until help arrives."

She felt his hand on her shoulder, and at that moment, she didn't mind. "I don't know what's wrong with me. This has never happened. Not even when Jackson's men attacked me."

"When did that happen?"

"This morning. After you called me." She dug her fingers into his forearm while she attempted to gain control of her ragged breathing and waves of fear.

"Today? Marlee, ordinarily, I might call this a flashback. But that would only be if the trauma happened years ago. You're in the throes of fresh trauma right now. Your mind hasn't processed what happened to you, never mind the bullets flying at you right now. Hang on. My team will get you out of here. They're good. Michael has always come through for me. Was there for me at my lowest point. I trust him with my life. He'll catch this guy, and we'll walk out of here today. And then I'll get you help."

Marlee thought of the odd look his friend had given her at the ranger station. She wasn't so sure this Michael guy would want to help her, but if Hunter believed in him, she would go with it.

"I walked out of that attack this morning without an ounce of distress," she said, remembering Jackson's early morning assault. "What's happening to me now? I can barely pick up my hand. I hate this. What if I'm ruined as an agent? This is all I know how to do. This is all I ever wanted to do. To beat this war on drugs. What if I'm out?"

"You're not ruined. You're not out. But it'll take time to move past this. Trauma affects us all in different ways." He paused. "But the fact that you're talking through it tells me you're going to be okay."

She noticed he didn't tell her to trust him. That would be the worst thing he could say, especially when they couldn't even see their shooter. And especially when he'd lost her trust a long time ago—and when he was a big reason for her going into this line of work.

"I bet you wish you hadn't called me now." Her words were more of a breath against his cheek and caused him to frown.

"I wanted the best. And you *are* the best. You'll get past this and be ready for service again. If I had known you were facing your own fight, I would have...well, I would have called for a different reason. Definitely not to pull you into mine."

"*Your* fight?"

"Case. I should've said 'case.'"

"You said this was personal. Why this little girl, Hunter? What's so special about her?"

Hunter grew quiet. When she thought he wouldn't answer her question, he whispered, "There's a chance she's my daughter."

Marlee gasped, more stunned now than when the bullets flew around her.

Hunter shifted to face her, turning on his side. He winced again and Marlee saw crimson spreading out on his tan jacket. *Blood.*

She pushed him down. "Hunter. The sniper didn't miss. You've been shot."

"I know." His smile was weak and less than humorous. "And he's not done with us yet."

As if on cue, another round of bullets sprayed the surrounding dirt.

Hunter's concern for Marlee spiked his adrenaline while the bullets flew. He had felt the hit when he went down, but his focus went to Ben's little sister's ashen face. Something was going on with her, but he also would be no good to her if he bled out. Libby whined beneath him, sensing his injury as well. Gustav's fur rippled under Marlee, the dog eager for his next command from his handler. Hunter knew the German shepherd would guard her with his life if something happened to him. She'd trained him well.

"Help is on the way," he said, pressing his shirt tightly over the wound. "Just stay low until they get here. Stay with your dog."

Marlee reached her free hand to push his away. Her other hand still held her gun, but no longer at the ready.

And no longer trembling.

"You could be dead by then. We need to keep pressure on it and can't let dirt inside the wound." Her hand pressed firmly over his, strong and sure. She was steady once again as well.

"It's just below my ribs on the right. I really don't feel much pain. Just a stinging."

She shifted onto her side and moved his hand, feeling to his back. With intense determination on her face, he was glad to see the color return to her cheeks. Just a few moments ago, her stark-white complexion had concerned him more than any bullet wound. Her vacant expression had alerted him to a wound in her that he couldn't see to do anything about. He felt useless to help her.

"You're looking better," he said, though she gave no inclination of hearing him. Purpose now drove her as she leaned close to inspect his wound.

"No entry." She sighed with relief. "The bullet grazed your waist right below the rib cage. You might be bruised." She pressed harder, not letting up.

"I can handle it, Marlee. Thank you." Hunter covered her hand to let her know he would take it from there.

She glanced up to meet his gaze, and he watched the moment she realized she had been helping her number one enemy. Her eyes blinked twice, yet she didn't retract her hand from beneath his.

Car engines roared, closing in, but neither of them moved.

The K-9s whined and shook beneath them, reminding them they had work to do and a child to find, but when deep sadness crossed Marlee's face, Hunter saw the pain his past actions still caused her.

"I'll never be able to fix what I did," he said. "No matter how hard I try."

"No, you can't," she said. "Not ever."

Car doors slammed. "All clear!" Elliott hollered from the road. "Hunter! Are you here? The scene is clear. The guy's on the run!"

Hunter prepared to shout their location but needed to voice his concern for Marlee's well-being.

He studied her. "If I had known you were struggling with trauma effects, I never would have asked you to come. I know you won't talk to me about it, but I think you should talk to someone."

Marlee pulled her hand from his side. Blood stained her skin as anger flashed across her face. "Too bad you never told Ben that, instead of buying him his drugs." She pushed to her knees. "We're over here! Gustav, come." She stood, climbing out of the crevice to be seen by the rangers, waving them over. Her dog settled beside her as Libby remained with Hunter.

Elliott and Michael rounded a boulder and rushed to them.

"Hunter! Don't move." Michael knelt by his side.

"I'm fine. Just a graze. Nothing to worry about. We're both going to be okay. Right, Marlee?" Hunter's question settled on the desert breeze, calming the tension between them.

He would keep her secret…for now.

"Right," she whispered, dropping her attention to Gustav.

"The shooter took off in a truck when we approached. Sheriff Hawkins is tracking it right now," Elliot informed them as he scanned the scene for bullets. "We need to get you to the hospital."

"Not yet," Hunter said. "Libby found something."

Michael helped him up, and Libby immediately returned to the place she had been tracking before the gunshots. She sat to alert him to something in the six-foot lote bush.

"She's tracking," Marlee said, moving close to the bush with Gustav. She passed Hunter, but he sidled up beside her, wincing and gripping his left side. They reached for the same branch to push apart, their hands touching.

"Thank you for not saying anything," Marlee whispered, keeping her hand beside his. "I'll be okay. I promise."

Hunter studied her profile, not entirely believing her. "Interesting. That's exactly what Ben said when I asked him to talk to someone as well."

Marlee gasped, catching his gaze and pulling her hand away. Regardless of what she thought, he *had* told Ben to get help. And as far Hunter knew, Ben had listened.

Sadly, Ben didn't live long enough to follow through.

Hunter bent to splay the large lote bush's sharp branches open for a better view inside. Thorns cut into skin and scraped up his arm as he used it to widen the branches more. "I hope I'm not making another mistake by keeping your secret, too."

Marlee knelt to peer into the bush with him, whispering harshly, "They are hardly the same thing."

"Until someone is hurt or killed because of it. Then they're not." A splash of rainbow colors protruded from the dirt. "Bingo. Nice job, Libby." Hunter jutted his chin at the team. "Over here! Libby found Nancy Sue's second sneaker. She must have hidden herself in here. Most likely cut herself up doing it, too. These are sharp little daggers. Poor kid. She must have been so frightened."

Marlee grabbed a thorny branch, carefully keeping it still with two fingers. "Look what else Libby found. DNA."

A clump of curly brown hair knotted among the thorns, torn straight from the child's scalp…or the killer's.

FOUR

"Get the hair to the lab," Marlee instructed a deputy as she passed the evidence bag over to him. "And bring out the crime scene investigators again. They've now missed evidence in both areas." She'd yet to search the entire meth dump site and could only hope they hadn't botched any other leads. Gustav would sniff them out anyway, but he'd have his work cut out for him. "Let us know when you have an ID on the hair."

She glanced at Hunter, who was looking at the clear evidence bag of hair. He gripped his side in obvious pain. "You should get to the hospital. I can handle searching the rest of the site."

He stared after the bag with a pensive look as the deputy walked to his cruiser. Hunter's strange melancholy triggered the memory of him telling her that Nancy Sue might be his daughter. In the aftermath of seeing him shot, Marlee had mentally tabled that shocking announcement.

She deadpanned as she spoke low for his ears only, "A simple cheek swab would alleviate your curiosity." Marlee held her tongue about asking Hunter's reason for not knowing he had a child in the first place. If Nancy Sue was his child, then what was the deceased mother, Donna Hartman, to him?

Hunter caught her gaze. "I just need to focus on finding Nancy Sue. I'll treat this like any other search and rescue. I can't let anything personal get in the way." Hunter glanced over his shoulder. Michael and his dog, Zeke, searched other bushes. Hunter lowered his voice. "I doubt I'm the father. Donna would've told me. She wouldn't have been that callous to keep that from me."

Or she kept it from you, and you killed her for it.

Marlee held her tongue and led Gustav toward the dump site. "Did you give her a reason to keep the information to herself? Did you conveniently forget to call the next day?" Marlee pressed her lips tight, following her shallow remark, especially when Hunter's face paled. "I'm sorry. I shouldn't have said that. It's none of my business. We discuss the case only, just as we agreed."

Except this information could be crucial evidence in the case.

Hunter could be a suspect.

They walked along the canyon wall in uncomfortable silence, each letting their dog take the lead along the trail, tracking their expertise. Libby had already earned her treat for the day with her find in the lote bush. Now it was Gustav's turn to show off his skills.

The K-9 walked briskly with his nose to the ground, excitement rippling the black-and-tan fur down his back. Suddenly, he stopped and sat on his haunches, black eyes alert.

"I take it this is the dump site," Marlee said. Even with the trash bags gone, Gustav had sniffed out the spot by residual evidence of chemical waste. "It'll be a long shot if he can detect anything that would give us a location of the production. I'll need to go through the bags in the lab."

Hunter led Libby away to stand by a place of overturned earth. "Even if he finds a lead, doesn't mean the meth dealers have the child. The trash could have already been here. Perhaps that's what Donna was investigating."

"You think she came here for a piece?" Marlee pondered the idea. "Makes sense. I assume as a reporter that's something she typically did."

"Yeah, all the time. It came between us a lot…and why she broke it off. I was working a child-smuggling case and getting ready for the raid. She overheard me on the phone." Hunter led Libby to another spot, leaving Marlee to figure out Donna had beaten the police unit to the location to get her story.

"Did she blow the case?"

"The smugglers were long gone by the time we arrived. Two years of work down the drain. The same with our relationship. I was going to marry Donna. We were engaged."

So, Marlee had heard correctly through the law enforcement grapevine. "I had heard you were getting married. I assumed you tied the knot."

Hunter shook his head. "I wanted to try again, but rebuilding our trust wasn't working. I was afraid to share anything with her, and she made it clear she was going for the big-time. But then one night she showed up on my doorstep, crying. She apologized and said she loved me. I thought we were making a turn and…well, one thing led to another."

Hunter dropped his gaze from Marlee's. His cheeks flushed in obvious embarrassment. "I really thought we would make it work. But the next morning, she was gone. Slipped out during the night and left her engagement ring on the kitchen counter. That was six years ago. After that, I had to watch the woman I loved go after her journalistic dreams from afar. Eventually, she landed the six o'clock slot on Channel 11, while I hit rock bottom. Even left the force, feeling like it was law enforcement that killed my relationship. I lost my way, but thankfully, Jesus forgave me and led me to search and rescue. And now, here I am." Hunter displayed a forced smile that showed no joy in all he'd just shared with her.

"And here you are…bleeding from a gunshot wound when you should be at the hospital. But instead, you're putting your life on the line. Do you always give these searches your very last breath?"

"Always. I failed to rescue my best friend when his very being screamed for help. Every person found alive atones for the second-biggest mistake of my life."

"Second?" *What could be worse than causing Ben's death?* Marlee led Gustav across the desert floor, each crunch of sand pebbles echoing beneath her steps, competing with that blaring question. What else had this man she used to moon over done? She stopped in front of Hunter. "Please do share. What was your first-biggest mistake, Shelton?"

Hunter's hazel eyes glittered a myriad of colors, and without blinking, he said, "Lying to you."

Hunter watched Marlee stride ahead with Gustav, her determined focus set to avoid any talk of their past. How could he make amends with her if she wouldn't let him apologize? And what if she did let him say he was sorry? It didn't mean she would forgive him, anyway. When Hunter had given his life to Jesus, the weight of his choices had been lifted off his shoulders, but some of his choices still left his heart heavy.

Yet none as much as the one where he'd lied to Marlee about Ben's addiction.

"I don't think the investigators came down this far," Hunter said, leading Libby along the trail Marlee and Gustav took and letting Marlee have her way…for now.

"Their mistake. Gustav says there's something here." Sheer pride filled Marlee's voice.

Hunter smiled, letting Libby come up beside the K-9 to join the hunt. "You have a great dog. But I can tell by your trust in him, you already know that."

"He's the best. I raised and trained him myself."

"Then the credit goes to you. Ever thought of going into training?"

Marlee gawked with a sideways glance. Her expression reminded him of when they were younger. She was such a sweet kid, even if she was a tagalong. She'd made it tough to lose her, though Ben had his ways to convince her to go home, especially when…

Hunter suddenly realized Ben would always make sure Marlee wasn't around for the parties through high school and college. Not even when Marlee followed them to the same university. At the time, Hunter hadn't noticed, his only concern being for which cheerleaders would be present at the events. His sole focus on girls had caused him to miss Ben's growing addiction to the drugs being passed around. Then Ben was cut from the college football team for possession in his locker, and there was no bringing him back from his problem after that. But being a part of the Texas football phenomenon meant joining the spirit of unbreakable bonds. It meant family and unspoken oaths. Even after Ben was cut, Hunter stood by those bonds, never realizing his confidentiality would lead to Ben's death in his senior year of college. But somehow Ben had known he had a problem and protected Marlee from finding out.

Why didn't I see that until now?

Gustav snorted, tracking faster, reminding Hunter about their current grim task and the clock ticking with each passing hour to find Nancy Sue. The scent of clay mixed with metal hit his nose instantly, causing him to cover his nose. The sound of insects buzzed louder with each step across the hard-packed earth.

Marlee asked, "Did Donna always go after the most dangerous stories?"

"Aren't you more concerned with what that smell is?"

"I know what it is. And so does Gustav. It's death. Putrefaction mixed with ammonia. I've smelled it many times when users have overdosed and their so-called friends dump their bodies. But two dead bodies in this park also tell me something else was going on. Something dangerous brought Donna here. So what was the story she was after?"

Hunter scanned the trail ahead but saw nothing. Then Gustav turned right off the path, and after four more steps, sat on his haunches. A woman's legs protruded from a bush, and by the bloat and smell, her death hadn't just happened. The heat could speed up decomposition, but Hunter figured the murders had been close together in time. Two women killed here in the same time frame. That wasn't a coincidence.

The gaseous odor clung to the canyon air, mixing with the bitterness that swirled inside Hunter. Donna had always chased danger. Was Marlee right? Had the chase finally gotten Donna killed? And had it put an innocent child—*his* child, maybe—at risk?

Hunter exhaled sharply, forcing the thought aside. "I'll call Sheriff Hawkins."

Marlee pulled latex gloves from one of her cargo pants pockets. She knelt, running her gloved fingers through the branches to reveal the bloody corpse of a woman. Her dirty clothes reeked of ammonia along with her body's decay.

"She was a meth user. I think." Marlee examined the woman's face. "Her clothes tell me that story, but I won't know for sure until the autopsy."

"It's obvious she was stabbed, just like Donna."

"Still want to know what drugs were in her system." Marlee stood and removed the soiled gloves, turning them inside out. "If Donna had planned to expose a meth operation out here, she was bound to make enemies. Maybe she got too close.

Maybe she witnessed this murder and was chased down to receive the same treatment."

Hunter swallowed the lump in his throat. "That sounds like Donna." His voice came out hoarse. "She didn't just report on crime—she hunted it."

"Looks like she became the hunted."

Hunter huffed, anger growing in him. "She never let up, never stopped until she had the full truth, no matter the cost. I can't believe she brought her daughter with her."

Marlee looked up at him. "That's what doesn't make sense."

A stiff silence stretched between them, the weight of uncertainty pressing hard. Marlee dusted off her hands. "We need to check Donna's house. If she was working on something big, there might be notes, recordings—anything that could tell us what she uncovered before she died." Hunter hesitated. "Donna's house…" He shifted, the throbbing in his side growing worse. "She also might've left information for finding Nancy Sue."

Marlee nodded, and Hunter exhaled, gritting his teeth through the burning pain and the dread of going to Donna's house, to the life she chose over him. "Yeah. Let's get this over with."

Even as he said it, trepidation coiled in his gut. As they turned back toward the vehicles, Hunter glanced down at Libby. The loyal SAR dog watched him with steady, unwavering eyes, sensing the turmoil in her handler. He gave her a reassuring scratch behind the ears. "Let's go find some answers, girl."

Even if those answers were to questions he'd long since buried.

FIVE

The hour-and-a-half drive, after a trip to the ER for Hunter, brought them to the outskirts of San Antonio. Marlee, Hunter and their K-9s arrived in Hunter's K-9 SAR Unit truck at dusk. Leaving the dogs in their secure kennels, Marlee and Hunter approached the steps to Donna's small white house laden with yellow tape left by the investigators. The porch was empty besides a flowerpot that had been tipped over, spilling its soil on the floorboards. It struck Marlee as odd at how the sparse place barely reflected the glamorous life of a news anchor. There also wasn't any evidence that a child lived there. No chalk drawings on the sidewalk approaching the steps or a bicycle lying in the front yard. The scene felt cold, even without knowing the woman had been murdered.

Hunter hesitated at the front door. Having been cleared to enter, he unsealed the tape, but his hand then hovered over the handle. Marlee didn't miss the tension in his jaw or the slight tremble in his fingers.

"First time back here since the breakup?"

He shook his head. "I've never been here."

Marlee jolted. "Seriously?"

"We always met at her apartment in the city, or she visited me at my home outside the park. I worked at a ranch then and lived on the property. I own the ranch now. But this place belonged to her father. After her mother passed away, he sold their large house for this. Not too long after, he died of a heart attack and left this place to Donna. She had just graduated from college and said she wasn't tied to it. She never invited me here. Said she liked the idea of living on the ranch. Or so I'd thought."

Marlee wondered about the place Hunter called home and if she would see it while in the area. She pictured big rooms to fit his broad stature and warm colors to match his mild temperament. It also dawned on her she needed to find a place to stay that night when they returned to Harmony.

Hunter released a deep breath and pushed the door open.

Inside, the house was neat but lacked warmth. The white walls were bare except for a few shelves in the living room, where pictures of Donna's loved ones and her recent journalism award stood proudly displayed in the center. In the kitchen, stacks of mail cluttered the table, some envelopes unopened, others bearing the bold red print of Past Due notices. Marlee slipped on latex gloves and picked up one from a law firm.

"She was in some kind of legal battle," she murmured, flipping the envelope over before placing it back down. "I wonder what for."

Hunter didn't respond. He stood in the center of the living room, his gaze scanning the space with a quiet intensity. Then, as if shaking off whatever thoughts had held him still, he moved toward a desk in the corner.

Marlee walked past him and down a short hall, into what she assumed was Donna's bedroom. Unlike the rest of the house, this room had personality—soft lavender curtains, a vanity cluttered with expensive perfumes, and a stack of books on the nightstand. One caught her eye. It looked more personal, with blue bonnets on the spine. She flipped it open and skimmed through the pages, her pulse slowing as she realized what she was reading.

Donna's diary.

Marlee nearly closed the book out of respect for the deceased. The blue satin ribbon opened the book to Donna's last entry two months ago. Flipping the pages back, Marlee could see she'd written sparingly lately. Turning more pages, Marlee landed on entries from five years ago.

Nancy Sue is here, and I never thought I could love another human being as much as I love my daughter. Her father and I couldn't be happier.

Marlee nearly snapped the book closed, not wanting to be privy to this knowledge. This book needed to be brought to the police. There could be information in it to help solve Donna's murder.

It definitely solved the paternity of Nancy Sue.

But instead of closing the journal, Marlee flipped back a few more pages until she saw Hunter's name scrawled on the page. Donna's words brought more questions than answers. She wrote about Hunter not being good for her. Marlee frowned and wondered what the woman meant.

"Find something?"

Marlee jumped at Hunter's soft, almost reverent voice behind her. "You scared me."

He filled the doorway, eyeing the book. "What's that?"

She pulled the book close, not wanting to let him see what Donna had written about him. Some things were best not known. What would be the point of hurting his feelings? Marlee thought it strange that she was worried about his feelings, wondering where that came from, but she did. She didn't want him to read this.

"It's Donna's diary. Just some old stuff in here, but the detectives should have it, just in case there's a lead." She hoped he would let it go.

But Hunter stepped into the room, taking the book from her reluctant hands, his face unreadable as he skimmed the page she had been reading. The entry she had stopped on was dated six years ago—right around the time Donna had left him. She had just read the words before he entered and winced, knowing he was about to be hurt by them.

Leon understands me in ways Hunter never will. Maybe if Hunter had been a better person, I wouldn't be in this mess.

Hunter's grip tightened on the book, his throat working as he swallowed. "Leon?" His voice was hoarse.

Marlee hesitated, then pointed to the framed photos on the dresser. Several showed Donna with a tall, rough-looking man with piercing dark eyes. Some were older, but a few were recent. One had Donna, the man—Leon, she assumed—and a little girl sandwiched between them.

Marlee exhaled slowly. "Looks like Donna and Leon were a thing. And if these pictures mean anything, it's been going on for a while. It also means…he could be Nancy Sue's—"

"I know what it means." Hunter pressed his lips tightly after cutting her off. "Sorry. I… Just give me a second to process this. I guess it makes sense why she ended things. She had another man she loved more. Someone…better."

He remained silent, his expression impassive, but Marlee didn't miss the subtle way his shoulders dropped, as if some quiet hope had been snuffed out. Donna might have been unfaithful to him, and that had to hurt. Or perhaps Hunter was let down over not being Nancy Sue's biological father. Had he wanted Nancy Sue to be his?

Marlee placed a hand on his arm, an instinct she quickly second-guessed and removed. "I'm sorry, Hunter."

He blinked, as if her words pulled him from his thoughts. "It was six years ago. I was a different person. I was still the person you knew back then. Reckless. I'm sure you'll agree that she was right. It was best to end it." He picked up a photo of Donna and Nancy Sue, sitting on a swing together. He opened his backpack and dropped it inside.

Marlee held her tongue about removing items from a crime scene, but still glared a warning at him.

"Something with Donna's scent…for Libby."

Except they weren't tracking Donna.

Marlee let it go and shifted her focus back to the case. "Let's figure out why Donna was chasing this drug ring and find her daughter, whom she loved very much."

They spent the next thirty minutes going through papers, opening drawers, looking for anything that connected Donna's death to the investigation she had been pursuing. But they found nothing else in her bedroom that would lead to a story she was chasing.

"Perhaps there's something in her office at the television station. Some notes or a phone log."

Hunter led the way out of the room but stopped in the hall, looking at the second bedroom door. The name Nancy *Sue* was written in a child's hand on a pink piece of paper and taped to the door. He paused only a heartbeat before entering.

In the middle of Nancy Sue's pink-and-white bedroom, Hunter paused. She watched as he crouched and picked up what appeared to be a well-loved teddy bear from the floor with his gloved hand.

"Libby can use this." His voice was steadier now, his resolve returning. A good sign, but he masked his true feelings. "Whoever clocked me in the head made off with Nancy Sue's items that I was using to give Libby her scent. With this, Libby might have a stronger smell to track."

Marlee removed a plastic bag from one of her cargo pockets for the toy. She accepted Hunter's professional reason but also noticed that bringing the child her toy was something he needed to do for her. He cared about the child, his or not, and that painted him in a different light than Marlee remembered. "Nancy Sue's also probably missing her stuffed animal and will want it when we find her. And we *will* find her, Hunter."

Marlee heard the compassion in her voice, but hesitated to say more. His earlier statement about the man she once knew him as, reckless, as he dubbed himself, did conflict with the man she stood with now. She found it harder with each passing moment to find the Hunter from eight years ago, the man who inadvertently caused her brother to die. Where was that careless man? Could a person really change that drastically?

Before she could ask, his phone buzzed. He answered, and Sheriff Hawkins's voice carried through the line. "Hunter, we got an ID on the other body in the canyon. She wasn't a user. She was an undercover narcotics officer. Detective Adrianne Fowler out of Austin. She'd been infiltrating a nomadic meth lab operation in the area and was working it from the inside as a worker. Someone must have found out and her cover was blown."

Marlee felt her eyes widen at the horror of the idea. Hunter's stunned expression showed he was drawing the same conclusion. A cop was Donna's source? Marlee grabbed his arm as he lowered the phone.

"Donna went to the canyon to meet her, didn't she?" Marlee spoke her thought aloud.

Hunter's jaw tightened. "Looks like it. Which means Donna's source wasn't just any informant—she was a cop."

Marlee exhaled, the weight of the discovery settling in. "And someone made sure they both paid the price for it."

Hunter gripped the steering wheel tightly as the Texas Hill Country rolled past in the darkness. Without a warrant, getting into Donna's work office at the television had been met with a closed door in their faces. The mousey girl working late hadn't felt comfortable letting them inside. But she'd told them how to get a hold of Leon Carl, the man in Donna's life, so it wasn't a completely dead end. The girl also told them the two of them weren't together anymore. But she said the man was Nancy Sue's father.

"Do you want to make the call to Leon and tell him his daughter is missing, or shall I?" Hunter spoke into the dark cabin of his K-9 SAR truck with the dogs sleeping soundly in the built-in kennels behind them.

Marlee chuckled. "How about we let Sheriff Hawkins handle that message? You don't really want to call the man your fiancée left you for, do you? Even *if* their relationship ended since then."

"True."

The soft hum of the engine filled the silence between them, only adding to the weight of the past two hours since they left the station. The air between them had shifted, less tense but still thick with unspoken thoughts. All Hunter wanted to do was air out their past once and for all. But Marlee had made it clear they would only talk about the case.

"You sure you don't want to stay at my ranch?" he asked again, breaking the quiet. He'd invited her when they started the drive back, but Marlee wasn't having it. The motel in town was fine with her, so she said. But Hunter still carried the pain and stitches from that morning's ambush. He could only assume the shooter was someone from the meth lab, trying to take them out before they found more evidence. But Hunter hadn't forgotten Marlee had other dangers knocking at her door. "It's safer for you than the motel in town. Clint Jackson is still out there, and if he finds out your location—"

Marlee sighed. "I can take care of myself, Shelton."

"You forget, I saw your residual trauma this morning. Ordinarily, I would say you've got this, but we just don't know that for sure right now. Besides, it's not just you. It's Gustav, too." He shot Marlee a sidelong glance. "You really want to put him in unnecessary danger?"

She pursed her lips, staring out the window. "You fight dirty."

"I fight smart." Hunter smirked, knowing he found the way to Marlee's heart. Her dog.

She exhaled heavily, then nodded. "Fine. But only because my dog's safety comes first."

Hunter chuckled. "I'll take the win."

They lapsed into silence again, this time more comfortably. Marlee shifted in her seat. "So, when did you buy the ranch? No offense, but I never figured you for the rancher type."

He grinned. "Neither did I. But it turns out hard work and fresh air beat drowning in regrets. And taking care of horses is therapeutic."

Her gaze softened in the dashboard's glow. "Ben would've liked that."

A pang of sadness tightened Hunter's chest. "Yeah. He would've. And he would have loved the ranch. It would have been so good for him." When she didn't respond, Hunter continued, "Bought the ranch five years ago." His voice carried a note of fondness. "From the man who introduced me to Jesus. I worked security on the Double Fork part time after college, renting a cabin on the property and helping Owen even after I became a cop. I wanted nothing to do with God then, but Owen was patient." Hunter chuckled, thinking of his old friend. "I changed to full time during my year off from the sheriff's department, after the mishap with the smuggling case. Then Owen needed to sell. He gave me a deal I couldn't refuse—a friend and savior in Jesus *and* first dibs on the Double Fork."

"Where's Owen now?"

"Moved to Colorado to be closer to his grandkids. He checks in now and then, but more to chat about faith than the ranch. He's a good friend. He filled a hole in my heart after Ben."

Marlee frowned.

"Is there a problem with that?" Hunter asked.

At her silence, he figured the conversation was over. Apparently, both Ben *and* God were off-limits for conversation. "I won't keep quiet about God. Not after everything He did for me, and the pit He pulled me out of. What Donna said about me was true. You should know that more than anyone. I let your brother, my best friend, die out of obligation to him and fear for what would happen to me, instead of being honest about the life we were living and forcing him to get help."

"Stop."

Hunter sighed but refrained from saying more. They needed to have this conversation and fix things between them, even if they never saw each other again after she went back to Houston. They both needed to say what they needed to say to each other.

Marlee put her hands on her knees, hesitating before saying, "You were Ben's hero. Even when you two fought, he looked up to you."

Hunter swallowed past the lump in his throat, grateful Marlee was willing to talk about Ben, but he hadn't been expecting that. "I wish I'd been worthy of that, but I wasn't. Marlee, I was afraid of getting kicked off the team like he had been. I kept his secret to cover my own sins. I thought I was helping him, but I only made it worse."

They lapsed into silence again. Then Marlee spoke. "Donna wrote you weren't a good person. What did she mean by that? Did she know about these...*sins*?"

Hunter tensed, his knuckles whitening on the wheel. "Yeah, she found out I had commitment issues and went out with a lot of girls," he admitted. "I met her at a college party. She said she wanted to do a story on me for the college paper. She was so different from all the others who just wanted to...make out. I think Donna did her research, though, and found out I was more of a player off the field than on. Still, her article was kind, and we started dating seriously after that. I really wanted to change and treat her differently. I was always faithful to her, but old girlfriends kept coming back. Right after I joined the sheriff's department, I asked her to marry me. I think I asked her more to prove I'd changed than for love. But she said yes, until one day soon after she ended it, saying there were things in my past she couldn't get past. I just assume she was talking about...all the girls. I didn't blame her. I didn't like myself, either. As Owen said, I needed Jesus. And he was right. I really changed after I believed."

Marlee studied him, shaking her head. "This is all so crazy. I had no idea. I only remember good things about you. Two college football players on top of the world. Back then, I thought you and Ben would go pro. Well, until he was cut in his senior year. I was shocked."

Hunter glanced at her with a shake of his head. "Ben protected you from the life we were living by pushing you away. He never let you see the truth. I realized that today. He was protecting you, even while I thought I was protecting him. He was right to keep you out. I wasn't." Hunter exhaled deeply. "Man, I miss him."

She hesitated before responding, her voice quieter. "If you had another chance right now, what would you do differently?"

He huffed. "I ask myself that all the time. I like to think I would have carried him kicking and screaming to rehab, but I probably would have first told him Jesus loves him. Really loves him. Every part of him, good and bad. He knows it all and still loves us." Hunter nodded, then glanced her way. "*Then* I would have carried him kicking and screaming."

At first Marlee was quiet. Then her laugh filled the cabin, first soft and deep, then loud and contagious. She quieted again before saying, "He really protected me?"

"Yeah, he did."

"I think he would want me to forgive you."

Hunter felt something shift inside him at her words, stunned with hope. But before he could respond, headlights flared in the rearview mirror. Hunter barely had time to react before a truck slammed into them, the force sending their vehicle skidding off the road.

"Hold on!" Hunter shouted as the world turned upside down.

SIX

Marlee's ears rang from the impact, her vision swimming as she tried to make sense of the world tilting sideways around her. The truck landed nose-down in a shallow ravine, the front windshield spider-webbed with cracks. The distant screech of metal settling groaned through the night.

Then came the barking.

Gustav and Libby.

The dogs were alive. Hopefully, they were unharmed. Marlee sucked in a breath and turned to Hunter. "You good?"

He grimaced but nodded, rubbing a hand over his face as if trying to clear the haze. "Yeah. You?"

"What happened?"

"Someone slammed into us and pushed us over."

Marlee's breath hitched. Three attacks in one day? First Jackson, then a sniper from the meth lab, and now some random driver?

Doubt it.

She might even say these were all Jackson and his men and knew what was coming next.

Before she could give a warning to duck, the first gunshot cracked through the night. The bullet struck the passenger door with a metallic clang, jerking her fully into the moment.

"Move!" Hunter shouted, already reaching for the glove compartment where he'd stashed his firearm.

Marlee fumbled with her seat belt, adrenaline kicking in. "The dogs—"

"Get them," Hunter ordered. "I'll cover you."

Another shot rang out, this one shattering the side mirror. Marlee shoved open the door and scrambled toward the rear of the truck, pulling open the kennel door. Gustav and Libby were snarling, their bodies poised to jump. Their instincts were sharp—they knew danger was near but weren't afraid of gunfire, part of years of training.

Hunter fired back into the darkness, his gun flashes momentarily illuminating the night. Shadows shifted among the trees above them, the unseen shooter keeping their distance but pressing their advantage.

"Come on, girl," Marlee muttered as she unlatched Libby's cage. The bloodhound leaped out, instantly alert. Marlee did the same for Gustav, and the German shepherd bounded free with a low growl. His thick fur rippled.

"They're out!" she called.

"Run! Go left! Through the trees," Hunter yelled, firing off another round before retreating.

Marlee didn't hesitate. She turned and bolted down a narrow path, the K-9s flanking her, their breath hot in the chilled night air. Marlee gulped deep breaths to fill her lungs, causing the powerful aroma of Ashe juniper trees to fill her senses with their resin and piney spice. Hunter was beside her, his gun still gripped in his hand, his head swiveling to check their six.

Behind them, boots crunched through gravel.

"He's close," she warned. All she could think was Jackson had found her. She removed her Sig from her waist, readying it for when she could get a clear shot at the drug lord.

Hunter shouted, "Keep going!"

Branches whipped against Marlee's arms as they plunged into the underbrush, the terrain growing more uneven and rocky. The path narrowed with more dense clusters of trees. Another gunshot drowned the distant sound of an owl screeching, this bullet zipping just past her shoulder.

"Down!" Hunter shoved her forward. She hit the ground hard, rolling with the impact as another shot whizzed overhead. The dogs whined, circling her protectively.

"We're sitting ducks here!" she panted, feeling the same anxiety she'd experienced in the last gun assault. "We need cover."

Hunter's eyes darted around, calculating. "We're closer to my ranch than I thought. If we can make it—"

Another shot drowned out his words.

Marlee's chest burned as she sucked in air. "How far?"

"Half a mile."

Half a mile? It might as well have been ten.

Hunter shifted, then looked at the dogs. "We need a distraction."

She caught on to his idea, nodding in agreement. "You want them to throw off Jackson?"

"You think this is Clint Jackson?"

"It's exactly what he did to me before I left Houston. Pursued me and started shooting. Hunter, he won't stop until Gustav and I are dead."

The moonlight shadowed Hunter's face, displaying his processing of the idea. "Okay, the dogs are our best shot."

Marlee swallowed hard, then crouched beside Gustav, stroking his thick fur. "You up for a little misdirection, big guy?"

Gustav huffed, ears perking.

She made a sharp hand signal, and Hunter followed her lead with Libby. Both K-9s took off in opposite directions, their footfalls nearly silent. The movement in the dark was enough to draw the shooter's attention. More bullets fired—aimed at where the dogs had just vanished.

"Now!" Hunter yanked Marlee up, and they sprinted toward his property.

The minutes stretched unbearably as they ran. Each breath burned in her chest, her boots skidding over loose gravel as they rounded a bend. Then, finally—a light, way off in the distance.

Hunter's ranch.

The ranch house stood on the hill like a beacon, the porch light casting long shadows. Yesterday, she would have laughed at the idea of running toward his home. But now, she saw something so wonderful. Safety and strength...but hadn't she always seen that in him, and that's why his choices hurt so much when he hadn't lived up to those qualities, not only with Ben's addiction...but also on the night she went to tell him how she felt about him?

He had humiliated her.

"Almost there!" Hunter touched her shoulder, strong and reassuring.

But now she knew Ben would want her to forgive his best friend. Marlee wasn't sure she was capable. Eight years of anger and pain still had its grip on her. But what if they didn't make it out of this assault alive? Did she want to die with unforgiveness in her heart?

Behind them, heavy footfalls pounded closer. Their pursuer had realized the trick with the dogs and had tracked them instead. Another shot whizzed by her, slowing her steps as she ducked her head, noticing the dogs coming back around. She couldn't let them get shot. Neither wore vests.

Marlee risked a glance back—and saw the man running from inside the trees.

A masked figure, silhouetted against the moonlight, rifle raised.

Why would Jackson bother covering his face? She knew what he looked like. She had an entire file on the criminal.

She also knew he never worked alone. Most likely, he had men strategically placed throughout this juniper forest. That man might be one of them and not Jackson at all. There could be more up ahead.

Or this shooter was someone else entirely. Could their attackers be part of the meth lab—aligned with the men who had Nancy Sue?

Marlee clenched her teeth, pivoted and fired her own gun, forcing the shooter to drop low. Hunter grabbed her arm, yanking her toward the house. The dogs were back now, snarling as they closed in on the threat.

"Go, go, go!" Hunter shoved her toward the porch steps.

Marlee nearly collapsed against the door, fumbling for the handle as the dogs created chaos behind them. Finally, the door gave way, and she and Hunter tumbled inside. He whistled for the dogs to run his way. Just as they entered the house, Hunter turned and fired one last shot, then slammed the door. A bullet struck the wood just as the lock clicked into place.

Panting, Marlee pressed her back against the wall, heart pounding. She took a deep breath to calm her nerves. It sickened her over having no control of her rising fear. She needed to beat this setback.

If she made it through this night alive.

Outside, silence reigned.

Hunter exhaled roughly, running a hand through his damp hair and waking up his phone. "Don't get too comfy. It's not over yet. But I won't let anything happen to you. I promise. I'm calling for backup."

Marlee locked her gaze on him, on the man she'd held such

contempt for and now had to trust with her life. Her heart raced as she realized nothing was ever fair when it came to him.

But could she forgive him while she still had breath in her lungs?

Another spray of bullets hit the hard wooden door. Out here in the middle of nowhere, it would be at least thirty minutes until helped arrive.

Before she could blurt out the words she wanted to say to him, someone picked up his call, and he turned away to relay the emergency.

An assault in progress…while her tongue stuck frozen in her mouth. And not even another onslaught of rapid fire could thaw it.

Hunter checked the locks and dead bolts on every door and window in the house. His pulse continued to pound in his ears and adrenaline still coursed through his veins. He returned to the great room to see Libby and Gustav pacing restlessly near the fireplace, their ears twitching at every sound outside.

Marlee stood a few feet away by the unlit fireplace, arms crossed over her chest. The moonlight played across her face, highlighting the tension in her clenched jaw. She'd said little since they'd burst through the door, but the way she kept looking toward the window told him she was still on edge.

"You all right?" he asked.

She nodded stiffly. "Fine."

She wasn't. He wasn't, either. They had just been ambushed, run off the road and hunted through the dark like prey. But Marlee's walls were up, and Hunter knew better than to push.

A sharp knock sounded at the door, making them both flinch. Libby let out a low growl, her body tensing.

"It's the sheriff's department," a familiar voice called from the other side.

Deputy Willis.

Hunter glanced at Marlee before unlocking the door. Two uniformed deputies stood on the porch, Willis and Montgomery, their flashlights illuminating the darkened landscape behind them.

"Area's clear," Willis said. "We found your truck down in the ravine. Looks like the shooter ran back to the road and took off. No sign of him or another vehicle."

Hunter exhaled, though the relief was short-lived. The danger hadn't passed, not really. Just for the moment. "Thanks, fellas."

The deputies nodded, lingering for a moment before Montgomery added, "I'm sorry this is all happening to you, Shelton. Wish it could be different. I know you and Donna were over long ago, but your relationship with her had set you on a better path. She was important to you, and we know it must still hurt."

Hunter pressed his lips tight, appreciating his old coworker's words. Hunter hadn't realized he'd needed to hear them. "That means a lot to me. Thank you."

The men turned to leave, but Hunter stopped them. "Hey, we found the identity of the child's father. Leon Carl."

Hunter gave the men all the information he had, as well as Donna's journal, for the murder investigation. Hunter shut the door and noticed Marlee turning away, arms still tight around her body. He could see the tension in the lines of her shoulders. The way she stood, rigid and distant, reminded him that this wasn't just any woman in his home. This was Ben's little sister. The same girl who used to follow him and Ben around like a shadow, wide-eyed and eager.

Except she wasn't that girl anymore. And he wasn't the same man, either.

"This wasn't Clint Jackson," he said, breaking the silence.

Marlee glanced at him. "How can you be sure?"

"Because someone tried to scare me off back at the canyon, before I even called you." He touched the back of his head where the bandage had been before he removed it earlier in the day. The lump was still there. "No, this isn't Jackson. This is about Nancy Sue. About the meth ring Donna was chasing."

Marlee didn't argue, which told him she probably agreed with him. Maybe.

Hunter ran a hand through his hair, knowing he must look a mess after that run for their lives. "Whoever this is, they want me to stop looking."

"Will you?"

Hunter met her eyes. "Not a chance."

She exhaled, her arms finally dropping to her sides. "Then we need to be smart about this. We need to talk to Leon Carl ourselves. See if he's connected."

Hunter clenched his jaw. The idea of speaking to the man made him uncomfortable because of his history with Donna. But Marlee was right. What if he was connected to the murder and abduction? That idea sickened him. How could a man do that to his own child? Hunter would cherish his children if God ever blessed him with some. Though, since he didn't date anymore, that was very unlikely.

Marlee studied him. "You don't want to talk to him, do you?"

Hunter shrugged, turning away. "It's not about what I want." Marlee saw too much in him. Too much of the truth. It made her a skilled agent, but he would need to guard himself more carefully, or she would know how much he longed for a family of his own...how he had once longed to be part of her family. Ben wasn't just a friend. He was a brother.

Silence stretched between them, thick with unspoken

thoughts. Finally, Hunter gestured down the hall. "Come on. I'll show you to the guest room."

She followed him through the house, her footsteps quiet against the hardwood floors. The ranch house had been his refuge for the past five years. The land was a place of solitude and healing for longer than that. The wooden beams overhead, the scents of cedar and leather—it all felt like home. But now, with Marlee here, it felt different. Smaller. More intimate.

He pushed open the guest room door. "You can stay here. Bathroom's down the hall."

She stepped inside, eyes scanning the space. "Thanks. Nice room." He was grateful she argued no more about taking him up on his offer. He would rest better knowing she was with him in his home. He ignored the thought that she was right where she belonged.

Hunter hesitated, watching her as she ran a hand over the quilt on the bed. The light from the bedside lamp cast a soft glow on her, illuminating the curve of her face, the way her hair fell over one shoulder. He felt something stir in his chest, something he hadn't felt in a long time for any woman, but especially for Marlee.

Attraction.

The realization hit him like a punch to the gut. This was Ben's sister. He had no business looking at her like that, feeling anything for her beyond old friendship. It was wrong. Disrespectful. Like letting Ben down all over again. Ben had always made it clear to stay away from his sister.

And Hunter had complied.

He took a step back, clearing his throat. "Get some rest. We'll regroup in the morning."

Marlee nodded, but something in her expression changed, speculative. She looked like she wanted to say something important, and he waited, giving her the time and space. But all she said was, "Good night, Hunter."

He nodded, turning and walking away, his pulse hammering in his ears. He told himself the knot in his chest was just exhaustion, the weight of the day pressing down on him. But deep down, he knew better. And that made him angry. At himself. At the situation. At the way Marlee had looked at him like he was someone she was trying to figure out all over again.

Hunter shoved the thought aside and made his way to his own room. But sleep wouldn't come easily tonight. Not with the memory of Ben in his mind and the presence of Marlee in his home.

And certainly not with a killer still out there, waiting for them to make their next move.

Hunter bypassed his bedroom and went to his gun closet by the fireplace, removing a rifle. He pulled up the rocker in the great room and settled in to keep watch in case the shooter returned.

The man had already taken one woman from his life and stolen an innocent child. Hunter wouldn't let the man get near Ben's sister. Not when Ben had done everything possible to protect her from the danger of this world, even from himself.

Libby and Gustav shuffled over and sprawled at Hunter's feet, drifting into their puppy dreams with ease. Hunter knew they might rest, but at a moment's notice, they would be ready to protect him with their lives.

Hours ticked by before Hunter allowed himself to close his eyes for a light doze. But unlike the K-9s, his mind wouldn't rest.

Donna cried out, "Leave us alone!" Her long red hair, always groomed to perfection, was now tangled in knots from when it had been twisted up in his fists. She escaped from him and lost some strands in his hand. She didn't dare stop running. Through the canyon, her breathing became ragged, fear etched into her face. She clutched Nancy Sue to her chest, her steps uneven on the rocky ground. A shadow loomed ahead, blocking her path. She froze, eyes widening as she pushed her daughter forward.

"Run," she gasped. "Don't stop."

Nancy Sue hesitated, but Donna shoved her away. "Go!"

The child disappeared into the night. Donna turned back toward the figure before her, her shoulders squaring as she whispered, "I was wrong. What have I done?"

A gunshot echoed in the canyon.

Hunter jolted awake, his breath sharp, his muscles coiled. His eyes adjusted to the sunlight streaming through the windows and skylights.

Marlee stood over him, his rifle now in her hands.

He blinked, still caught between dream and reality. "What happened?"

Marlee's expression was unreadable, her stance firm. "Get ready."

"For what?" Hunter straightened, shaking off the remnants of sleep.

She tightened her grip on the rifle. "We're going hunting for a meth lab today. SAC Williams just called. He gave me a lead on where I might find it. Gustav, come."

The K-9 barked in glee.

Hunter noted the intensity in her eyes as she added, "Time to go to work."

SEVEN

Hunter maneuvered his returned truck from the towing company, a little dented and beat-up but still drivable after being pulled from the ravine. Marlee, eager to check out the details SAC Williams gave her, instructed Hunter to take the next right as he drove onto the main road leading out of Harmony Village.

The early-morning light cast a golden hue over the hills, while Gustav and Libby sat in their secure kennels in the back, silent but alert. Marlee sat beside Hunter, straightening her posture with eyes focused on the road ahead. She pointed toward the state highway.

"It'll take us to the state park. That's where the narcotics officer's captain said the last known location of the meth lab was."

Hunter followed her direction, keeping his hands steady on the wheel, but his focus seemed to drift as she explained how SAC Williams was seeking more details to help them, working with the undercover cop's team.

"Are you listening?" she asked, studying him closely.

He blinked and shifted in his seat. "Yeah. Sorry. Just… I had a dream last night. Donna's voice is still echoing in my ears—her fear, her regret. I can't get it out of my head."

Marlee arched a brow. "You dreamed about Donna?"

"Yeah," he admitted. "She was running through the canyon, holding Nancy Sue. Someone blocked her path, and she told Nancy Sue to run. Then she said, 'I was wrong. What have I done?'"

Marlee was quiet for a moment. "What do you think she meant?"

"I don't know," Hunter said, gripping the steering wheel a little tighter. "It was just a dream. It wasn't real. There's no message or anything. But it's still bothering me. I never saw her so scared in all the time we dated. She feared nothing. No story was too dangerous for her to go after. Not even my story. She loved a challenge."

Marlee smiled at the way he described her, able and willing to admit to his faults. Before she think it through, she asked, "What did you see in her?" She inhaled quickly, covering her mouth. "I'm sorry. I shouldn't have asked that. Forget I said anything."

Hunter glanced at her, surprised by the question as well. "What do you mean?"

Marlee looked out the window, avoiding his gaze, cringing at her callousness and not sure she wanted to hear the answer to her own question, anyway. It was none of her business. "I mean…well, it's just…you loved her enough to propose. What was it about Donna that made you fall in love with her? You don't have to tell me, though. Really."

Hunter frowned, turning his attention to the road ahead. It was probably best if he ignored this topic of discussion and kept to the deal of discussing the case only, as she had asked. But when he glanced Marlee's way, she saw such sadness in his eyes.

"I didn't deserve her. And I didn't realize that until after she was gone." He sighed and faced forward again. "She was so strong. Smart. She had this fire in her—she wanted to change the world. But I guess I never really knew her. Or at least made her happy enough to let me join her."

Marlee held her tongue against any more slips. She stared at the road ahead, her fingers tapping restlessly against her knee, remembering the night she went to his apartment, the last time she saw him and felt his rejection. When she spoke, she kept her voice low and soft. "So you say you like women who are strong, smart and want to change the world. And yet, you turned me down."

Hunter turned his head slightly, obviously startled by her words. "What?"

She let out a quiet laugh, but there was no humor in it. "Do you remember right after Ben died, I came to see you one night? I had something to tell you. Do you remember?"

Hunter stiffened, and she knew he had recollected that night. And her words would not be welcomed for further conversation.

"I'm sorry," Hunter said. "I wasn't a good friend to you that night."

The memory, still so clear in Marlee's mind, brought back the feelings from that time in her life as if they were still so fresh. She had showed up at his apartment at midnight, grief-stricken and vulnerable. The way she had reached for him… Her fingertips still held the memory of touching the soft curls at the nape of his neck when she'd hugged him.

And then how he had pulled away just as another woman had called his name from his bedroom.

"Marlee…" he started, but she shook her head. "I wasn't a good person back then," he said anyway.

"You told her I was just a kid. You said, 'Ben's kid sister showed up.'" She turned to him then, his expression unreadable. "I know it was a long time ago, and I know I shouldn't care, but I did. Your words hurt. It took a lot for me to go to you that night. And then a few days later, I learned you knew about Ben's addiction, that you paid for the drugs that killed him. I realized I never knew you at all. And you never knew me. But to hear you talk about Donna like this…" Marlee shrugged, knowing she should end the conversation before she said too much. Before she gave too much of herself away. "I guess I didn't give you enough credit. I thought you were blind to seeing those qualities in a woman. But you were just blind in seeing them…in me."

A stunned expression came across his face as he shook his head. "That's not true. I always knew you were strong and smart," he said. "But Marlee, that's not what I looked for back then. I was treating women badly. I gave new meaning to the flavor of the week. I hurt them. In fact, I don't trust myself to date now. I'll wait for God to show me the right path, even if He never opens that door again. I'll accept that decision and be okay with it."

"Why?" Marlee didn't expect that response, and the air between them tensed as he turned the tables on her.

"Simple. For the same reason, I never went after Donna when she left me. I deserved to be alone after all the girls I left alone in my wake. After I left Ben alone in his pain. And Marlee, I didn't go after you that night because deep down I didn't deserve you, either. All you wanted was a friend, and I couldn't even do that for you because of my selfishness."

Marlee dropped her gaze to her hands in her lap. The cabin filled with uncomfortable silence now. She shouldn't have crossed the line with her question. Nothing good had come of it. It would have been best to let those sleeping dogs stay put.

After a few minutes, Hunter broke the silence with a low voice she had to lean in to hear. "I know you don't believe me, but I really thought I was keeping Ben safe. He told me his dealer was going to kill him if he didn't pay up. He owed a lot of money. I thought I was helping him stay alive." Hunter cleared his throat after it appeared he was holding back tears. "I didn't know he used the money to buy more. That those would be the drugs that killed him."

Marlee turned her face to the window, raw pain carving into her heart. No matter how many times she went over the events leading up to Ben's death, the outcome was the same. Would she ever heal and stop wishing for a different ending?

She would never get past this if she didn't.

Red rock signaled their approach to the state park. Hunter hit the blinker to turn onto the next road. "We're almost at the location your boss found. Not much out here this far from town."

Marlee relaxed into the purpose of her job. It's what always got her through the days, and she welcomed the work again.

She straightened and sniffed away the tears. Nodding, she said in her strongest voice, "That's why it's the perfect location to make meth. No one to call suspicious traffic or behaviors in to the police. We're here. On the right."

Hunter pulled off the road and parked his truck. But as he held the handle to his door, he paused and turned back to her. "I'll be making up for my behaviors for the rest of my life. But I still hope you see how much God has changed me for the better. I wish Ben had known about this amazing transformation. I believe he knows now, and I believe he would want you to know about it, too."

With that, Hunter exited to retrieve the dogs, while Marlee took a moment to regroup on how none of that conversation had gone the way she thought it would…or should. She had wanted him to take her pain away. Instead, she realized his pain was just as valid.

"You coming?" Hunter called, leashing Libby at the rear of the truck. "This place is a mess. Look. Discarded propane tanks, scorched metal sheets, empty chemical containers. And so much paper flying about. They moved out in a rush."

Marlee joined him at the back. Gustav leaped from the truck, his nose already to the ground, sniffing through the wreckage for the familiar scents of his job. Marlee pulled on a pair of gloves and hit the ground, running with him.

Hunter crouched low to the ground to inspect a canister while Gustav picked up various smells, finally latching on something and leading Marlee down an embankment. Below, he continued to sniff until he came to a pile of trash and sat.

Marlee sifted through and found tiny drug particles in a plastic bag. Inside were a few receipts. She squinted at the faded print on the paper and smiled.

"Nice work, buddy." She patted Gustav on the head, then called out to Hunter. "You hungry for breakfast? I hear Eggs and Griddles is a happening place."

Hunter stood to look down at her, his face twisted in disgust. "That's over in Lowry. And 'greasy spoon' is putting it nicely. Besides, we just got here."

Marlee held up the receipts in her gloved hand and headed back up the hill to show him. "Three receipts from the same diner. I'd call that a lead."

Hunter slowly grinned. "Ah, of course. The place must be a regular stop for them."

Marlee passed him on her way to the truck. "Let's go make some friends and get some answers."

Hunter grasped the steering wheel while he also grappled with the reality of never finding Nancy Sue. On the way down the highway toward the diner, his mind weighed with the possibility. Was she with these meth workers? Were they taking care of her, or had already killed her? The scorching sun beamed fully in the sky, casting golden light over the desert landscape, and all Hunter could feel was the suffocating pressure of time slipping away. Every second that passed without finding Nancy Sue was another second lost. Another second closer to never finding her at all.

He silently prayed this diner would be the lead to finding her. He then reached for his radio and checked in with his search and rescue team. “Talk to me. Any new leads?”

“Negative, boss,” came the response from Michael Gibbs. “We’re still sweeping the outer perimeter of the canyon, but so far, nothing.”

Hunter clenched his jaw. “Keep at it. Any sign at all, you let me know immediately.”

“Will do. Over and out.”

He set the radio back down and exhaled sharply. Marlee watched him, her expression unreadable. “You’re worried.”

“Of course I’m worried,” he admitted, his voice rough. “We’re pushing nearly fifty hours since she went missing.”

Marlee nodded. “That’s why we have to make this stop count. The receipts we found prove the meth lab crew frequents this diner. Someone here knows something. We just have to get them to talk.”

Hunter didn’t reply. He just pressed his foot harder against the gas pedal.

The diner sat in a mostly abandoned strip mall, its neon Open sign flickering in the front window. It looked like the kind of place where the coffee was burned, and the regulars had been sitting in the same booths for decades. As Hunter parked, he noted the handful of rusted trucks and beat-up sedans in the lot.

The moment they stepped inside with the dogs at their heels, every head in the place turned toward them. Conversations died. Mugs were lowered back onto saucers with slow, deliberate movements. A thick tension filled the air.

Hunter exchanged a look with Marlee. "Friendly bunch."

She kept her voice low. "Yeah. Let's see how much they like talking to a federal agent."

"You might want to keep that information on the down-low for now."

"Aw, announcing that is my favorite part of the job." She winked his way, sweet and strong, as always.

Once again, Hunter found his thoughts weren't brotherly.

He quickly recovered and strode up to the counter to slide onto a stool beside a man hunched over his coffee. The guy didn't acknowledge him, just kept stirring his spoon in slow, circular motions.

Libby sat at attention beside him.

"Morning," Hunter said jovially. He eyed the newspaper that the man had splayed open on the counter. "What's the news? Anything good?"

The man closed it, but not before Hunter saw he was reading about the two murders in the canyon.

"Real sad about those women. Wouldn't you say?" Hunter continued.

Behind him, he heard Marlee and Gustav approach another table. The lone waitress was pouring coffee for the customer.

"You wouldn't happen to know the customer of these receipts, would you?" she asked.

"No, ma'am. I can't tell that from a receipt." The waitress, without so much as a passing glance at Marlee, retreated to behind the counter.

Marlee followed with Gustav. "You didn't even look. There are some credit card digits visible. Surely you can check your books to see if the entire number is listed. I can take it from there. That wouldn't be too difficult, would it?"

The waitress set the coffeepot back on the burner. "You'll

have to come back when the owner is here. I can't help you. If you're not ordering something, you should leave."

"Who says we're not ordering something?" Marlee tapped Hunter on the arm. "I'm famished. Aren't you, too?"

Hunter asked the man next to him, "What's good here?"

The man got up and took his coffee to a booth.

"Tough crowd," Hunter joked as he saw the waitress slip through the swinging doors to the kitchen. At his nod, Marlee led Gustav in the same direction.

"Hey! You can't come back here!" The waitress's voice carried out to the dining room. "Especially with your dog. That's illegal."

Hunter and Libby stepped in behind Marlee. Before she could respond to the woman, a young man in his twenties bolted from the kitchen, shoving through the back door and out into the blinding sun.

"Gustav! Catch!" Marlee commanded, picking up her feet to follow her dog out the door.

The K-9 lunged forward, his powerful legs eating up the ground as he took off after the fleeing suspect. Marlee was right behind him, her boots pounding against the pavement and then the red sand.

Hunter passed Marlee, with Libby trailing behind him as he sprinted after the man. The guy was fast, but Gustav was faster. The dog closed the distance in seconds, launching himself at the suspect and knocking him to the ground. Gustav locked his jaw on the man's arm, sinking his teeth into flesh and keeping the man's writhing body in a painful hold.

"Get him off me!" the suspect yelled, exposing yellowed teeth.

Hunter stopped above the man with his gun drawn just as Marlee trained her weapon on the guy locked in Gustav's teeth.

"DEA! Don't move!" she shouted from beside Hunter.

"Oh, you're right, that *does* sound impressive," he said to her as she passed him the handcuffs with her free hand.

"See? I told you so." Marlee smiled sweetly, then commanded Gustav, "Off!"

The dog obeyed as Hunter crouched to slap the metal on the man's wrists. Gustav bared his teeth over the man, daring him to move one inch.

The smooth transaction impressed Hunter as he handcuffed the man, turning him over on his stomach. "You two work well together."

"Like clockwork." Marlee pulled the man to his feet in one swoop, spreading his legs wide to keep him in place. "How about you and me have a chat?"

The man stilled, panting, his eyes darting between them. He let a foul breath go Hunter's way.

Hunter cringed but shook it off. "You wanna tell us why you ran?"

The guy swallowed hard. "I—I don't want trouble."

"Then start talking," Marlee warned. "Because right now? You're in a whole lot of it. First question. What's your name?"

"I want my lawyer." The man spat in the dirt.

"For what? Did you do something wrong?" Marlee moved in close to the man's face. If his odor repulsed her, she didn't let on. Hunter thought that took strength all in itself.

"I've done nothing wrong. Let me go."

"All in good time."

Gustav growled, still baring his teeth at the man, causing him to squirm.

"Keep that dog away from me." His voice shook with panicked gasps.

Marlee gave a sharp whistle, and the K-9 backed off just enough to let the guy breathe—but not enough to let him think about running again.

Marlee spoke, her voice lowering into something smooth, coaxing. "Look, I know you're scared. But running makes you look guilty. Now, I bet you were just in the wrong place at the wrong time. Maybe you even know something that could help us. And if you help us, I can make sure that helps you."

The guy's beady eyes darted between them. "I—I know nothing."

Marlee sighed, shaking her head. "That's a shame. Because right now, you're looking at obstruction. Maybe aiding and abetting. Or perhaps an accomplice to two murders. But if you cooperate? We can talk about cutting you loose."

The man hesitated. Sweat dripped from his temples and his armpits. Then, with a nervous glance toward the empty parking lot, he muttered, "They moved the cook site again. Packed up two nights ago and went north…near the old mining tunnels outside of Grant Creek."

Hunter and Marlee locked eyes.

"That's all I know!" the guy insisted.

Hunter pushed the man from behind. "Guess what? You're still taking a ride with us. And you better not be lying."

Within moments, they moved him into the back of the cab—Gustav and Libby leaping in beside him.

"Guard," Marlee ordered and slammed the door shut. She moved to the passenger door. "Let's go," she said, climbing in.

Hunter didn't hesitate. He threw the truck into gear and drove off toward Grant Creek. Time was running out, and he picked up his speed.

"Thank you, Marlee. Because of you, we just might find her."

For the first time in this search, hope filled him, and he had this strong, sweet, beautiful woman beside him to thank for that.

EIGHT

Hunter floored the pedal to push the truck faster along the winding back roads. The surrounding landscape was wild and unforgiving, the rocky canyons and dense brush creating a natural fortress. Marlee sat beside him, phone in hand, coordinating with Sheriff Hawkins. The gruff voice of the sheriff filled the truck's cabin through the speaker.

"We're en route with backup. Got the girl's father with me," Hawkins said. "Leon Carl's been tearing himself apart since we picked him up. Says he'll do whatever it takes to get his little girl back. He wanted to join me, in case his daughter's there. She'll need to be comforted. But he's assured me he'll stay in the car."

Marlee met Hunter's gaze at the mention of Leon, and his jaw tightened. "Copy that," Hunter said. "We'll see you at the site."

He ended the call, exhaling sharply.

"You don't look too excited to meet the guy."

"Can you blame me? The idea twists my gut into knots. Donna most likely chose him over me and had a child with him. They even gave her the name Donna and I had talked about for our little girl."

"Really? You talked about those things with her?"

"Both our moms had passed. Her mom was Nancy, and my mom, well, you know my mom was named Sue."

Marlee remembered Hunter's mom. She had died of cancer when he was in high school. So much had happened to him in his impressionable years. Marlee wondered if perhaps Hunter's choices with all the girls were caused by his own trauma. Maybe even his choice to help Ben pay his debts.

"Do you still have your dad?" she asked, warily.

"Oh, yeah. You know my dad. Football is everything to him. He spends his retirement coaching elementary kids now."

"Not surprised. Gotta train the next generation." She joked but heard what Hunter wasn't saying. "He must have been angry when you refused to declare your intent for the draft. I think we all were."

He nodded. "Yep. Blew his top. It just wasn't as important to me as it was to him. And I didn't want to leave college early, not with Ben struggling… Anyway, it doesn't matter now. Nancy Sue is all that matters. *Her* future is all that matters."

Marlee frowned, not fully on board with his statement that his loss of a future in professional ball didn't matter. But she never realized he'd given it up for Ben. Stunned, she said, "Fair enough. Let's find her, then reunite her with her daddy."

Hunter grew quiet, and Marlee took the time to process all he had just said. There was so much she didn't know.

The location matched what their informant in the back had given up—a secluded creek bed tucked into a canyon's crevice, far from prying eyes. It was the perfect spot to cook meth. As they approached, Marlee caught sight of the battered old trailer, its windows covered with aluminum foil. The acrid scent of chemicals lingered in the air even from a distance.

As soon as Hunter pulled up, two squad cars rolled in behind them, red-and-blue lights flashing. Hunter climbed out and waved over a deputy. "Secure the guy in the back. Monitor him. We might still need what he knows."

The deputy nodded, moving toward the truck's cab, where their informant sat with the dogs watching him like sentinels.

Marlee's sharp intake of breath turned Hunter's attention to the second vehicle. Sheriff Hawkins stepped out first, but it was the man beside him that made Hunter freeze.

Leon Carl looked like he hadn't slept in days. His tanned skin was ashen, and his clothes looked like they'd been thrown on in a hurry. His eyes, bloodshot and wild with desperation, locked onto Hunter's. "Please," Leon said, voice thick with emotion. "Please, find my baby girl. I've already lost my beautiful Donna. I can't lose Nancy Sue, too."

Hunter nodded and said smoothly, "We're doing everything we can to find her." His ability to push aside personal feelings impressed Marlee.

Guns drawn, the officers surrounded the trailer. Marlee moved in first, Gustav at her side. Hunter followed with Libby, a jump to her step. The door creaked open under Marlee's hand, and from inside, the overwhelming stench of chemicals and sweat hit them.

Two men sat at a rickety table, their hands already raised in surrender. They were thin, gaunt-faced, with grime embedded under their fingernails. Their expressions of wide-eyed fear said they were only workers and not the big guns in charge.

Marlee switched to Spanish, her voice sharp and direct. "Where's the girl?"

The men exchanged glances and shrugged. "No niña aquí," one said. No girl here.

"I don't buy it," Hunter said, walking through to the back, pushing open the only closed door to reveal a filthy bedroom. He returned with a shake of his head at Marlee. Her gaze swept the main room, taking in the makeshift meth lab, more filthy bedding in the corner, the empty fast-food containers. And then—Libby let out a low bark, her body stiffening under the table. She ducked down, her nose working furiously, before emerging with a tiny pink jacket clutched in her jaws.

Marlee's stomach twisted as Hunter raced forward, taking the coat from his SAR dog.

"It's Nancy Sue's. I recognize it from a picture in Donna's house. And Libby's nose is never wrong. Nancy Sue was here. Recently."

Marlee turned on the two men. "Then where is she now?"

The room fell into silence, and Marlee knew she would make no headway with these workers. She instructed the deputies to take the men to jail and ordered the camper to be taken in as evidence. She also ordered a sweep of the area of a mile radius.

"Move your team over here," she told Hunter. "They are to be looking for Nancy Sue but also for any signs of remains or overturned earth."

At her direction, Leon's anguished cry from outside sent shivers up Marlee's spine. A glance at Hunter showed his own shoulders folding in and a look of failure on his face.

As he had said, every rescue atoned for his past. If this rescue turned to recovery, Marlee wondered how it might affect Hunter.

Marlee took a steadying breath, pushing back the lump forming in her throat. She turned and stepped outside to Sheriff Hawkins. "This is still a rescue…until evidence says otherwise."

Leon let out a ragged sob. "Please don't stop looking. I beg of you. She's alive—I know she's alive!"

Marlee rested her hand on his shoulder. "We won't stop, no matter what. We will find her."

Marlee clenched her jaw, knowing that was not a promise

she should make. Her attention shifted to Hunter, joining her outside. He stood still, staring at the small pink jacket in his hands, his expression carved from stone. But beneath that, she could see it—the deep, gnawing look of failure. He had promised to find Nancy Sue, and now, with no sign of her, the weight of that promise was crushing him.

She stepped closer to assure him, too. She wasn't giving up. But before she could speak, a sudden roar filled the sky.

A helicopter.

Marlee shielded her eyes against the glaring sun but easily read the side of the chopper. It was a news helicopter, and moments later, dust clouds rose as news vehicles barreled down the road.

"Who notified the press?" Marlee demanded to know of those present.

Nothing but shrugs and denials came her way…until reporters stepped from the cars and thrust cameras and microphones at her.

"Agent Price, can you confirm if the child has been found?"

"What can you tell us about the meth operation you found here?"

"Are the two related?"

A female reporter with a bright smile and perfectly coiffed hair turned to the camera. "DEA Agent Marlee Price and her K-9 partner, Gustav, are heroes in this operation!"

A moment later, Marlee's phone rang. A glance at the caller ID showed SAC Williams was calling.

Backing away, she said, "I can't answer any of your questions in an active investigation. You'll have to excuse me." Marlee moved toward Hunter's truck. He covered her from behind until she was securely inside. He pushed back through the reporters, trying to get to the driver's door as Marlee answered her phone.

"Please tell me you didn't see any of that live?" she asked her boss.

"All of Texas saw it." Williams's voice was tight. "Agent, you just blew your location. Ready or not, Jackson will be on his way."

Hunter clenched his fists as the reality of Marlee's situation settled in. He stood at his kitchen counter while she sat at the table, her face illuminated by the glow of her phone screen later that day. Her jaw was set as she listened to SAC Williams on the other end, and the moment she hung up, Hunter could already tell by the steely glint in her eyes that she had no intention of leaving Harmony, no matter how dangerous things became.

"You need to go," he said, voice gruff, determined. "The marshals will take you somewhere safe while the DEA hunts down Jackson."

"I'm not running." Marlee shook her head with the same defiant gleam in her eyes that Hunter remembered Ben's little sister always having, no matter how much they tried to shake her off.

Hunter exhaled sharply, dragging a hand down his face. "Marlee, you found the lab. You did your part. Now, let the authorities handle this before you get yourself killed."

Her expression hardened. "And what about Nancy Sue? What about that undercover cop who gave her life investigating this ring? What about justice for Donna? I'm not walking away from this. I finish what I start."

Hunter felt his frustration coil tight in his chest. It was maddening—this need to protect her, to keep her safe. But Marlee wasn't a helpless civilian. She was trained, capable and fearless. And that only made his need to shield her more unbearable.

He forced himself to look away, pacing the terra-cotta-tiled flooring. Each step of boots drilled in the situation's heaviness. Marlee could have an army coming for her, and he doubted his abilities to stop them. The weight of past failures pressed on his shoulders.

"I left being a cop for a reason. I was better at search and rescue than protecting. What you did today, facing that man without an ounce of fear, it was amazing." Hunter stopped pacing and faced her. "But I fear I won't be able to protect you from Jackson and his men."

Her eyes widened in surprise at his confession. She stood from her chair, hands on the table. "If I ask you to try, will you?"

"Of course, but—"

"No cop is fearless, Hunter. We all must look fear in the face and try our best, anyway."

He shook his head. "But when presented with a safe solution, we need to consider taking the out."

Marlee frowned with a tilt to her head. On a sigh, she walked his way and placed her hands on his upper arms. It was almost comical, this woman a foot shorter than him, looking up at him as if she were the parent about to lecture him.

She implored him with a bright intensity in her eyes. "We're close. So close. We have leads."

"Which my team will look into. But I can't stand by and wait for Clint Jackson to take you out. That would be irresponsible of me as the head of SAR."

"Hunter, don't you get it? There will always be Clint Jacksons in my line of work."

He huffed. "Don't forget anyone with a grudge and a gun and in need of money. This isn't just about the case anymore. You know what that news broadcast just did. They're coming, and you're the target, Marlee."

Her lips pressed together, and she dropped her arms to her side and lifted her chin higher, locking her defiant gaze on him. "I've been a target since the day I put on my badge."

He stared at her, the fight in her eyes, the unshakable determination. His mind warred with itself. Protecting Marlee had been instinctual, automatic—born out of loyalty to Ben. But now, standing here, he knew it wasn't just that. It wasn't just guilt. It wasn't just an obligation. It was something deeper, something far more dangerous than any enemy lurking in the dark.

He wasn't supposed to feel this way. Not about Marlee. Not about any woman anymore...until God opened that door again.

And He never opened that door with Marlee.

Hunter stepped back, his pulse hammering in his ears. Fisting his hands at his sides to keep from enveloping her in his arms. "You need to go. For both—"

Her phone buzzed in her hand. She glanced down, breaking the moment between them. Hunter exhaled sharply, taking another step away, reaching for the counter to stabilize himself. He needed to get his head on straight.

"It's SAC Williams again," she muttered. "Probably to tell me to stop ignoring his orders."

She declined the call and tucked the phone away. Hunter studied her, conflicted and exasperated all at once. "You're impossible."

Marlee smirked. "And yet, you still keep trying to tell me what to do."

A strained chuckle left him, humorless and dry. "Yeah, well, someone's got to keep you alive."

"I can do that myself. I'll be ready. I promise."

Silence stretched between them. The teakettle she'd put on whistled through the kitchen, but she didn't move.

Was she waiting for his approval?

Hunter turned and removed the kettle, giving her his back. He rubbed his neck, trying to shake the tension winding through him. When he turned to face her again, he felt ready. But then Marlee stepped close and took his hand, and in an instant, his breath caught.

She was staring at him—not with defiance, not with frustration, but with something else. Something warm and inviting. Something that made Hunter's heart hitch.

Genuine caring reflected in her eyes. Caring for *him*?

"I don't want to leave," she admitted, voice quieter now. "Not just because of the case."

Hunter swallowed hard. "Marlee..."

She squeezed his hand. "Listen to me. You were always so important to me. I know you considered me a leech."

Hunter shook his head but chuckled at her choice of words.

She flashed a sweet smile. "Don't even try to deny it."

"We just wanted you safe. Ben and me. We wanted you safe. I still do. No matter the ocean of issues between us."

"And I want that ocean gone. It hasn't served either of us well, wouldn't you agree?"

Chagrined, Hunter nodded.

"Good, then I want you to look at me and really see me. Not Ben's little sister running on your heels. Not even DEA Agent Marlee Price. If you met me today with no knowledge of history, what would you see in me?"

Hunter dropped his gaze to where she held his hand. Closing his eyes, he drew on the takedown at the diner, at the way she stood her ground with the press and the ways she'd given orders to Sheriff Hawkins on the next steps of the rescue. Even how she'd comforted Nancy Sue's father.

"If I had never met you before today, I would say you are brave, strong, capable and compassionate."

Her sweet smile returned. Slowly, she let go of his hand

and reached to cup his cheek. Standing on her tiptoes, drawing her face close to his.

Hunter's pulse roared in his ears.

"Do you know how long I have waited for you to see me?" she asked.

"I've always seen you."

She shook her head. "Not like this. Thank you for those kind words."

"They're the truth. You are all those things…and more."

"And so are you, Hunter Shelton. But you're also empathetic. You didn't fail as a cop. You just hadn't found your way yet. But you have now. Be proud of that."

"Thank you," Hunter whispered, barely restraining himself from leaning in to kiss her. He felt his world tilting on its axis, or maybe that was his head in the clouds. "God led me the whole way."

Marlee pursed her lips, doubt clear on her face. On a sigh, she closed the gap between them, but her lips never touched his. Instead, they landed on his cheek while she patted the other.

"If that's what's you believe, then why do you think He won't lead me, too?"

She was across the room, heading out, before Hunter could fumble a response. Was he really doubting God not to lead Marlee?

"Gustav, come," she called to her K-9 from the doorway of the great room. "We have preparations to make." She sent Hunter a backward glance. "Jackson surprised me once. He won't succeed again. I'll be out in the barn setting up a perimeter of security if you need me. But no more talk of me leaving."

And with that, she was gone, taking the warmth right from the room…as well as the oxygen.

Hunter's knees buckled, and he released a breath he hadn't

realized he'd pent up. He couldn't deny the direction of his thoughts when she had been so close to him.

Hunter had wanted to kiss her. To kiss Marlee Price, *Ben's sister.*

And he still did.

This wasn't how it was supposed to be. He shouldn't want her like this. He wasn't supposed to feel like this about her or *any* woman. Those days were behind him.

But he *did* want her. And that made her presence in his home even more dangerous.

Just thinking about kissing her raised Hunter's heart rate.

"This…this can't happen," he muttered, shaking his head as if that would undo his thoughts. He grabbed the back of his neck again and squeezed. "Not now. Not ever. God help me. Because as long as she's here, I'm not only going to need Your guidance. I'll need Your strength."

NINE

Marlee stood in the barn, tightening the last length of rope she had strung between two wooden posts. It wasn't much, but it would serve as a simple trip wire in case anyone tried to sneak onto Hunter's property in the dead of night. She had spent the last hour using whatever barn tools and materials she could find to create barriers and obstacles, crude but effective security measures. If Clint Jackson or whoever was behind the killings came for her or Hunter, she would not make it easy for them.

She wiped the sweat from her forehead and glanced toward the house, where a faint light shone through the window. Hunter was inside, likely still pacing, still brooding over her refusal to leave Harmony. He thought she was being reckless. Maybe she was. But she wasn't about to walk away now, not when Nancy Sue was still out there.

Her phone vibrated again. Marlee sighed, already knowing who it was. SAC Williams had been calling relentlessly, trying to persuade her to let the US marshals take her to a safe house. But she wasn't leaving. Not yet. She ignored the call, shoving the phone back into her pocket before moving toward the workbench.

Hunter was finally seeing her for who she was—not just Ben's little sister, not just the girl from his past, but a capable, intelligent agent. Someone who could hold her own. That thought alone kept her grounded, even as exhaustion weighed heavily on her limbs.

The phone buzzed again, and this time, the number on the screen was unknown. Marlee hesitated. If it was another one of Williams's tactics, she was going to let him have it. But something inside her told her to answer.

She swiped the screen. "Agent Price."

A low chuckle sent ice down her spine. "Hello, Marlee."

Her breath caught in her throat. Clint Jackson. His voice slithered through the speaker like a snake in the grass. And suddenly, she wasn't in Hunter's barn anymore. She was back in that shootout, back in the chaos, her ears ringing from gunfire, her hands shaking as she fought for her life. The residual effects of his attack were still so fresh, and now they crashed over her in a suffocating wave.

"Surprised?" Clint taunted.

Marlee forced herself to breathe, to shove past the icy grip of fear clawing at her chest. "How did you get this number?"

"I have my ways."

"What do you want?" She kept her voice steady, unwilling to give him the satisfaction of knowing he had rattled her.

"I know where the girl is."

Marlee's heart slammed against her ribs. "You're lying."

"Am I?" Clint chuckled again, the sound making her skin crawl. "You're smart, Marlee. Smarter than the rest of them. That's why I called you first. I can tell you where to find her, but I need something in return."

Her grip on the phone tightened. "And what's that?"

"You. Alone. No backup. No dogs. Just you and me, sweetheart. I'll tell you everything you want to know."

Marlee's mind raced. It was a setup. It had to be. Clint would not hand over Nancy Sue's location out of the goodness of his heart. If she went alone, she'd be walking into her own execution. But what if he was telling the truth? What if this was the only way to find the girl before it was too late?

She exhaled slowly. "Where?"

"That's for me to decide. You'll get a time and place soon. Just be ready."

The call ended, leaving Marlee standing there in the barn's silence, her pulse roaring in her ears. She lowered the phone, her fingers trembling slightly before she clenched them into a fist.

A shadow shifted near the doorway. Marlee turned sharply, her hand instinctively reaching for her weapon. But it was Hunter.

His face was unreadable, but she could tell by the way his jaw was clenched that he had heard enough.

"No," he said firmly.

Marlee crossed her arms. "You don't even know what I'm going to say."

"Yes, I do. And the answer is no."

She exhaled sharply, frustration bubbling inside her. "Hunter—"

"No," he repeated, stepping toward her. "You are not walking into a trap alone. I won't let you."

She hated how his protectiveness made warmth bloom in her chest, how the worry in his eyes made something deep inside her ache. But she couldn't let him get hurt because of her.

"If something happened to you because of me, I would never forgive myself," she whispered.

Hunter stared at her for a long moment before shaking his head. "If something happened to you, Marlee, I wouldn't survive it."

Her breath caught. There was something raw in his voice, something real and unguarded. It left her speechless.

Hunter reached out, hesitating for only a second before he cupped her face in his callused hands. His thumb brushed against her cheek, and she leaned into his touch before she could stop herself.

"I'm not letting you go alone," he said, voice low and firm. "We do this together. Or not at all."

Marlee wanted to argue. She wanted to tell him it was too dangerous, that she had to do this on her own. But looking into Hunter's eyes, she knew there was no changing his mind.

And maybe, just maybe, she didn't want to.

Hunter stepped out of the barn, the cool night air doing little to ease the tension still buzzing through his veins. He needed space, needed clarity, but the moment he set foot onto the gravel drive, headlights swept over him as a car pulled onto the ranch. The hum of an engine followed the crunch of tires before the motor cut out. The headlights stayed on, illuminating the driveway.

Michael Gibbs climbed out first, stretching as he surveyed the property. Right behind him, Charlie Woodridge adjusted her ranger's cap, her dark ponytail swaying as she shut the door and moved toward him.

"Hey, Hunter," Michael called, holding up a small, dirt-covered toy in a plastic bag. "We think we found something today."

Hunter's focus sharpened instantly, his gaze zeroing in on the object. It was a tiny stuffed rabbit, its once-white fur now stained with mud. His gut clenched. "Where'd you find it?"

"About three miles from the park's entrance," Charlie answered, stepping forward. "Near one of the lesser-traveled trails. Thought you might want to see if Libby could track it. To see if it matches the scent of Nancy Sue's other personal effects. My dog didn't track it, so don't get your hopes up. But perhaps Zeke has lost the scent. We're going on days now."

"I have another stuffed animal from Donna's house. Let me grab that and get Libby."

Just then, footsteps sounded behind him, and Marlee emerged from the barn. She wiped her hands on her jeans, looking between the three of them with curious eyes.

Michael's expression shifted the moment he saw her, surprise flickering across his face. "Marlee? I thought you'd be long gone by now."

Marlee flipped her palms up and shrugged. "Still here."

Michael shot a look at Hunter. "Why?"

He was a little surprised by Michael's animosity toward Marlee. Then he remembered Michael had been around to witness Marlee cut him off after Ben died. Hunter made a mental note to talk to his friend afterward. It was time for them all to let go of things in their past.

Hunter kept his voice even. "I invited her. She's helping with the rescue."

Michael's jaw ticked, and Hunter thought he might need to pull his friend aside right then and there to have that conversation. He didn't need Michael to defend him. He needed him to stick to the job.

"She found the lab," Michael pressed, eyes narrowing. "What else is there for her to do?"

Marlee stiffened, but before she could respond, Hunter cut in. "We still have a missing child. How about we focus on the reason you're here?" Hunter said.

Michael exhaled, shaking his head. "I don't want to see you like before, man. When you needed the Price family, Marlee made sure they were off-limits."

Marlee inhaled sharply. She turned to Hunter, guilt flickering across her face. "I—" She hesitated, then sighed. "I was young and couldn't see past my pain."

Hunter didn't want to go down that road. Not now. He gestured toward the stuffed rabbit. "Again, let's focus on what you came here for. Let's see if this is Nancy Sue's."

Charlie, shifting uncomfortably in the growing tension, cleared her throat. "Right. If Libby can confirm it's Nancy Sue's, then we know where to search next."

Hunter walked into the grass and crouched to place the toy on the ground. He glanced back at Marlee. "Would you grab the stuffed bear from her house? It's in the truck."

As Marlee did as asked, Hunter called for Libby, who was lounging on the porch. She ambled down the steps, tail wagging and ready to do her master's bidding.

Marlee disappeared inside the truck and returned a moment later, not only with the stuffed bear but also with the pink jacket Libby had found at the meth lab. Hunter let the dog take in the scent on the bear. Her ears perked up as she processed the information. He then gave the command, "Seek."

Libby's nose dropped to the ground, her body going rigid before she moved forward, sniffing in slow, calculated movements across the driveway, then the lawn. A moment later, she halted, her tail wagging, and gave a sharp bark.

Hunter's heart pounded. "That's a match."

Charlie let out a breath of relief. "Then we know where to look."

Michael stepped forward, his skepticism replaced with focus. "I'll radio the others. We start at first light."

"Wait," Marlee said, walking in the opposite direction. She put the coat behind a rock. "I want to confirm this is Nancy Sue's jacket. Then we'll know she was at that meth lab."

Hunter commanded Libby to seek again, and while his SAR dog did her thing, everyone waited on bated breath. Slowly,

Libby sniffed around until she picked up the matching scent. From there, she made a beeline for the jacket and sat.

Collective breaths released.

"It's drug-related," Marlee said, latching her gaze on to Hunter. He could see her mind spinning to make some sort of connection with the evidence. "Donna was seeking a story. She and the undercover cop were murdered. Someone at the lab took Nancy Sue with them."

"And now?" Michael asked. "Where is she now? What would they have done with her?"

"Sold her to the highest bidder." Marlee's blunt response was one no one wanted to hear. But Hunter knew she was thinking Clint Jackson was that buyer.

Marlee's phone buzzed in her pocket, pulling Hunter's attention to her lit-up screen. She turned it away to check the message, but her face went blank. If it was another message from SAC Williams, she would have shown annoyance or something. But she gave no reaction, and Hunter figured it was Clint Jackson following up with his directions to her.

His gaze sharpened as he caught a flicker of alarm in her expression. "What is it?"

She hesitated, then quickly locked her phone. "Nothing."

Hunter wasn't fooled. He captured her gaze with one word. "Marlee."

She exhaled, looking toward Michael and Charlie, then back at Hunter. "I would rather talk about where this toy was found. Do we have coordinates of the location?"

Michael frowned. "Yeah. Why?"

"May I have them?" Marlee held an annoyed edge in her voice at Michael.

Michael looked at Hunter and sighed before checking his phone to rattle off the latitude and longitude.

Marlee made a groaning sound under a release of breath.

"Talk to me, Marlee," Hunter said and exchanged a look with her, a silent understanding passing between them. The location Clint just sent her was a match or close to it.

Clint knew. Somehow, the drug lord had a connection to the kidnapper. It made sense that he would know everyone running drugs in Texas, maybe even beyond.

Hunter clenched his jaw. "Then I guess you'll have your way, Agent Price. If Clint Jackson really knows where Nancy Sue is, we have no choice but to meet him."

"*We?* No way. Just me." Marlee bypassed the group and went inside the house.

"Who's Clint Jackson?" Charlie asked.

Hunter felt a headache coming on. "The man who wants Marlee and Gustav dead."

Michael huffed a bitter laugh. "She did him wrong, too, huh?"

Hunter glared at Michael. "Let it go. We all need to work together."

"She's the one who needs to go." Michael stepped up to meet his gaze. "Whether or not you want to believe it, her presence is putting all our lives at risk. You're asking us to stand in the line of fire. Because when the bullets fly, and they will, those men won't care who takes a hit. Are you ready for that fallout, boss?"

TEN

Marlee adjusted the strap of her tactical vest and tugged her jacket tighter against the early-morning chill. The sky above was a deep indigo, lightening slowly as the dawn hours passed into daylight. The entire search and rescue team, along with Sheriff Hawkins and his deputies, were scattered across the terrain in a traditional grid-search fashion, their voices echoing intermittently through the vast wilderness as they called Nancy Sue's name.

Marlee kept Gustav on a short leash as she stepped carefully over the uneven ground, her boots crunching against gravel and dry brush. Hunter walked beside her with Libby, the two of them moving in practiced sync. Though they had spoken little since last night, she could feel the tension rolling off him in waves. Every second that passed without finding Nancy Sue weighed on them both.

Still, Marlee's mind wasn't entirely on the search. Her phone, tucked securely in her pocket, felt like it was burning a hole through the fabric. She was supposed to meet Clint at 7:00 a.m. She'd told no one. Couldn't tell anyone. It was a risk—one she had to take alone. She expected Clint to trick her and she doubted he had the child as he had claimed. He wouldn't want a kidnapping charge, and she would make sure he got just that.

Marlee cast a glance at Hunter from the corner of her eye. He was sharp, observant. If she wasn't careful, he'd figure out what she was up to before she had the chance to slip away. She slowed her steps and reached for Gustav's leash. "Hunter?"

He glanced at her. "Yeah?"

She hesitated. "Can you take Gustav for a while?"

His brows furrowed. "Why?"

She offered a tight smile, not willing to lie to him but also keeping the information on a need-to-know basis. "I don't want him in the line of fire if something goes wrong. I don't want any of you taking a bullet when I'm the target. I overheard what Michael said last night. And he was right. I chose not to go into a safe house, but I won't bring the risk to any of you."

Hunter stopped walking. His expression darkened. "And what about you, Marlee? You're willing to put yourself at risk?"

She felt the weight of his stare and forced herself to hold steady. "I can handle myself."

His jaw flexed. "You don't have to do this alone."

Marlee inhaled slowly, then handed him Gustav's leash. "For the safety of all, I do. If I need backup, I'll make the call. The meeting location is right over the next hill. I need intel on who Jackson has partnered with. Let me do my job, and please, don't make a scene."

Hunter growled under his breath, and before he could argue, she turned and dashed away, weaving between the deputies as they continued their search. She could feel Hunter's eyes on her, but she kept moving, blending herself into the search until she saw her chance.

When Hunter was deep in conversation with Charlie Woodridge, Marlee veered left, heading toward a path that led deeper into the canyon. Her heart pounded as she moved with purpose, drawing her gun and keeping low. She was getting close to the coordinates Clint had sent.

A twig snapped behind her.

She froze. The hair on the back of her neck stood on end. Someone was tracking her. And not just one person.

Marlee surveyed her surroundings for cover, knowing what would come next.

The first shot rang out, followed by another, and another. Marlee dived behind a boulder, her breath coming fast as bullets spat sand into the surrounding air. The sharp cracks of gunfire echoed through the canyon, bouncing off the rock walls and disorienting her.

She gritted her teeth and forced herself to push past the rising panic. She had to think. Had to act. Shutting her eyes briefly, she inhaled deeply, forcing herself to calm the trembling in her limbs. She'd known she would head into target practice with her as the hunted. She needed to turn this fight around, and quickly.

Slowly, Marlee shifted her position, peering over the rock to get a better vantage point and set up her counterattack. Something strange caught her eye.

In the exact spot Clint had sent coordinates for her to go to, a body lay sprawled on the ground. Another murdered woman. A knife protruded from her back.

Marlee's blood ran cold.

If she went down there, she'd be exposed. An easy target. And if she turned back now, the shooter or shooters would cut her down before she ever made it back to the team. She was trapped with no one to blame but herself. But she wasn't out yet. She had her gun and ammo, and she wouldn't be out of this sick game until her very last shot.

Marlee zoned in on a path that led up to a higher vantage point. Her mind calculated the risk and figured she could take her best shots if she had the bird's-eye view. But the run would leave her exposed for a second or two. She would have to fake them out.

Marlee readied for her sprint while also shooting off a round in the opposite direction. Her shot pinged off a rock to her left. Immediately, gunfire followed, landing in the same place her bullet had. Marlee ran right at the exact moment, gaining cover just as the bullets tracked her previous steps.

With the protection of another rock, she had a few seconds to prepare for her run up to the top of the ledge. She studied the terrain and believed the piles of rocks would cover her if she stayed to the right side of them. She had to take the chance, knowing if she stayed put, they'd descend on her at any second.

She looked at the gun in her hand, only to see it tremble.

"No," she said to herself. "Get it together."

But saying it and doing it were two different things.

"God? No… I can do this on my own."

Without another thought, Marlee raced out of her spot and up the sharp incline, keeping her head low and her gun pointed toward the shooters. As she crawled over each boulder, she let them block her from view until she hit the top of the ledge and belly-crawled to the edge for her own target practice.

With the element of surprise, she took out one shooter who dared to step out from behind his tree. His cry echoed through the canyon before going silent forever. But immediately, the fire returned her way from what she could now deduce to be three more shooters.

She waited for another to move, giving her a clear shot, but she wasn't dealing with amateurs. The standoff brought an eerie silence, with only the soft wind and her erratic breathing conflicting with the panoramic view.

Had they run? Or would they catch her by surprise from behind? Marlee glanced around her location and saw only the one way up here. Making the move to go up had given her the best vantage point, but it also stranded her until the last three men were taken out.

Marlee remained low from her precipice, surveying the lay of the land far and wide. It wasn't long before she spotted Hunter and Gustav running up the trail. He must have heard the gunfire and come to her rescue. Because that was what he did. He rescued people.

Tears pricked her eyes at the realization that she had never truly seen him for who he was. He had tried to save her brother, standing by Ben even when his team had written him off. Hunter had been there, even if he believed he had failed Ben. He stuck by those he cared about.

And now, if she had just let Hunter stand by her, he wouldn't be running alone into danger.

She watched as he drew closer to the clearing where the body lay. Then, out of the corner of her eye, she caught movement—three flashes of light reflecting off something metallic. The three snipers were positioned in a triangle around the body. They had been waiting for her to approach, but she hadn't taken the bait. She'd known to run the other way.

But now, Hunter was in their sights and was coming into their line of fire.

Marlee's heart pounded. She had to act fast.

She pursed her lips and let out a sharp, commanding whistle. Gustav's ears perked up, and the dog immediately turned toward her position.

Hunter skidded to a stop, his gaze snapping up to her.

Then the guns went off.

The second Gustav darted away, Hunter knew something was wrong. The dog was highly trained—he wouldn't break away unless his handler called. And Marlee had called him. Which meant she was up there. And in trouble.

Then the first shot rang out.

Hunter passed Libby's leash to Michael and moved up the hill, hearing Michael shout his disapproval from behind. Sprinting toward the source of the gunfire, Hunter caught movement in the trees just before a second shot was fired. He threw himself forward, landing hard behind a large rock as another bullet zipped past him. His back flared with pain, but his vest absorbed the impact. The shooter had aimed center mass, which meant they were professionals. If he hadn't worn the vest today, he'd be dead. After the last shootout, he wasn't taking any more chances.

He exhaled sharply, shifting against the rough ground. He had to figure out where Marlee was, and fast. He scanned the terrain, picking up the subtle disturbances in the soil. Tracks. Hers. Leading up the incline to a ledge. She was up there. And judging by the sound of gunfire, she was pinned down.

Gritting his teeth, he focused on the layout of the area. He saw the body but couldn't let himself focus on her. That's what they wanted him to do. He had played football long enough to know how to read a field, and right now, this was just another game. He wasn't the biggest player, but he was fast and agile. He could use that to his advantage. If he could force the shooters to shift their positions, he might turn them against each other.

First, he had to move. He reached into his pocket, finding the tactical smoke grenade his SAR team carried for emergencies in case they found themselves lost. It wasn't military grade, but it would be enough to give him cover.

Hunter closed his eyes and counted to three.

Then he pulled the pin and launched it toward the tree line. The second the canister hit the ground and smoke began billowing out, he was in motion. Zigzagging through the open ground, he kept his body low, knowing the shooters would have to move to get a clean shot. Sure enough, more gunfire erupted, but this time, it was coming from multiple angles. Three of them meant three shooters. His plan was working as he'd hoped. The shifting visibility caused confusion, and one sniper mistook another's movement for an enemy target.

A single sharp shot rang out, followed by a grunt of pain. One down.

Hunter slid behind another rock, his breathing ragged as he assessed the remaining threats. Two left. He dared a glance up toward the ledge, and for the first time, he saw Marlee's silhouette against the backdrop of the sky. She had her gun drawn, and her stance was steady. She was watching. Good.

He needed her to see what he was about to do next.

Adjusting his grip on his pistol, he pressed his back to the rock and forced himself to think. The second shooter had repositioned, but he still had a clear shot at the clearing where the dead woman lay. If Hunter had stepped into that space seconds earlier, he'd be lying next to her.

He took a slow, measured breath and rolled his shoulders, the ache from the bullet impact reminding him to stay smart.

Hunter adjusted his stance and threw a small rock to the left. The sound of it skittering across the ground was just enough to draw attention. A split-second distraction.

Hunter moved.

With the agility of a wide receiver dodging a tackle, he sprinted right, leveling his gun as he went. The shooter saw him too late. Hunter fired two shots, striking the man square in the chest. The sniper crumpled without a sound.

Two down.

Hunter wasn't sure where the third was, but he wouldn't wait around to find out.

"Marlee!" he shouted, hoping she was still with him.

"I'm here!" Her voice was tight, but strong. Good. He had feared the gunfire would paralyze her again. She was getting past the trauma effects.

He risked another glance up and caught her signal. Three fingers. Third shooter was still active.

Hunter exhaled and scanned the landscape. The sniper had repositioned farther up, probably hoping to take Marlee out first.

Not on my watch.

He calculated the distance and knew he couldn't get there fast enough to take a clean shot. But he had one last play left.

He reached down, grabbing a fist-size rock. He locked eyes with Marlee one last time before he threw it hard, straight toward the shooter's blind spot.

The man shifted, looking away from Marlee for just a second.

It was all she needed.

The sharp pop of Marlee's gun echoed through the canyon. The sniper toppled backward, tumbling down the rocky incline with a sickening crunch. Silence followed.

Hunter sucked in a breath, the adrenaline finally catching up with him. Slowly, he stood, his body still thrumming from the fight. He turned his gaze back up to the ledge, where Marlee was already making her way down.

She reached him in seconds, her eyes scanning him for injury. "You hit?" she asked breathlessly.

"Vest caught it," he assured her. "I'm good."

She exhaled sharply, her hands shaking slightly as she holstered her gun. He could see it now, the aftershock settling in. Without thinking, he reached out, gripping her wrist. "Hey," he murmured. "You did good. You're getting past this."

Her gaze lifted to his, and for a moment, something unspoken passed between them. An old friendship that wasn't supposed to end.

Then Gustav trotted up to them, tail wagging like he hadn't just run through a war zone.

Hunter let out a breathless chuckle, ruffling the dog's ears before glancing toward the clearing at the dead woman's body.

"Looks like we found a third victim," Marlee murmured, following his gaze.

Hunter's jaw tightened. "They're keeping us from finding Nancy Sue. Stealing our time and resources."

Marlee nodded, her expression turning grim. "We need to figure out who the victim is and what she knew."

Hunter pulled out his radio. "Sheriff, we need a crime scene team out here. And we need to talk."

Sheriff Hawkins's voice crackled over the speaker. "On our way."

Hunter looked back at Marlee. "You still think going after Clint alone was a good idea?"

Her lips pressed together, but there was a flicker of something in her eyes—maybe regret, maybe something else. "No," she admitted. "But it gave us another body. And hopefully another lead."

Hunter sighed. He hated she was right. He also couldn't stay mad at her and ended up cracking a smile while reaching for her. He pulled her in for a hug, resting his chin on the top of her head.

"Don't do that again," he said.

"I won't."

"Really?" He pulled back to look at her face. "All it took was a shootout to make you see reason?"

She placed her hands on his cheeks. "No. All it took was my bird's-eye view seeing you come to my rescue and showing me how blind I've been."

Before Hunter knew what she was about to do, she planted a kiss right on his mouth.

Hunter remained still, absorbing this unknown territory with Marlee. Last night, he'd chastised himself for wanting just this, reminding himself it could never happen. But now here he was, letting it happen.

Suddenly, she stepped away, breaking their connection but still staring at him.

Hunter was at a loss for words, but needed to know why she'd done that. "That was…nice, but I'm not sure what it was for. Help a guy out?"

Marlee broke into laugh. "That was for Ben."

Hunter felt his eyes bulge out of their sockets. "Now I'm really confused."

Marlee laughed harder. "I mean, that was from me for what you did for Ben. For the steadfast friend you were to him. You may not have handled his addiction the way I would have liked. But your commitment to stand by him was honorable. Even after he was cut from the team and none of his family understood the extent of his problem, you remained his friend. I'm sorry I didn't see that until just now, when I watched you run into danger for me."

All her laughter left her eyes as they teared up, and suddenly, she was back in his arms, hugging him.

But Hunter didn't feel he deserved such accolades. He denied her claim for Friend of the Year, but caught sight of Michael running their way. In the same moment, Michael saw them and slowed his feet until he stood ten feet away.

"This is cozy," he said, irritation clear in his furrowed brow. "If you two are done, we'd like to check out the bodies."

Hunter nodded, letting Marlee slip out of his grasp. She swiped at her tears, smudging dirt onto her cheeks.

Sheriff Hawkins crouched at the woman while his deputies went to the dead shooters. "The killer left a note with this murder. Check this out, Marlee."

"Why's that?" Marlee moved closer, freezing after four steps. She read aloud, "'For Marlee.' What does that mean?"

Sheriff Hawkins turned the body to see the face, and Marlee gasped.

"The reporter from yesterday. The one who gave my location away. Someone killed her…for *me*?"

"You either have a fan…or it's a warning to you."

ELEVEN

Marlee sat at Hunter's desk, and frustration had her biting her lower lip. She speculated over a picture of the note left on the dead woman's body.

For Marlee.

The words felt like a taunt, a challenge issued by a killer who was always one step ahead.

The victim was the same reporter who had aired the footage, revealing Marlee's location. At first glance, it seemed like a message—a sick way of telling Marlee that the reporter had been punished for exposing her.

But Marlee wasn't convinced.

There had to be another reason this woman was dead.

Dragging Hunter's laptop closer, she typed the reporter's name into a search engine. Articles filled the screen, ranging from exposés on local politics to in-depth features of criminal enterprises. Nothing jumped out as an immediate connection to the other murders.

She drummed her fingers on the desk, thinking. Who was this woman outside of her career? Marlee clicked on the reporter's social media profiles and scrolled through her history. A few swipes in, a picture of a small group of women came up. The woman at the center had Marlee pausing mid-swipe.

Donna.

According to the caption, the reporter and Donna had once been roommates in college. They were both studying journalism.

Marlee inhaled sharply, her mind racing. She'd been operating under the belief that Donna had been investigating a drug story. But Donna wasn't an investigative journalist anymore. She was a news anchor. Her days of digging into dangerous stories were over.

So why had she visited the undercover agent in the first place?

Marlee pressed her lips tightly with a growing thought.

Unless Donna hadn't gone to see the officer for a story at all. The undercover cop might have died for a different reason.

A chill ran down her spine as the realization settled in. No undercover officer would blow their cover for a news segment.

But they *would* blow their cover to keep a child safe.

Marlee shot to her feet just as Hunter entered the room, a steaming mug in his hands.

"You ready for a break?" he asked, setting the tea down on the desk.

Marlee barely heard him. "The undercover agent blew her cover trying to get Nancy Sue away from the meth lab," she said, her words tumbling out in a rush. "She couldn't let them kidnap her or sell her or even kill her."

Hunter frowned, his expression shifting from concern to understanding. "And the reporter?"

"She was Donna's roommate in college," Marlee said.

Hunter exhaled and ran a hand over his jaw. "I remember little from those days," he admitted. "I was partying too hard. I met Donna at one of those parties, but I don't think I ever met her roommate."

Marlee studied him. For the first time, she saw a different

side of Hunter. Not the composed, controlled man he was now, but the reckless young man he had been back then.

She took her tea and moved to the couch, curling her fingers around the mug. "Michael implied I turned my parents against you." Her voice was quiet, tentative. "Maybe I did. They loved you like a son. And when Ben died, they lost both of you." She met his gaze, guilt tightening her throat. "I was young and angry. I never should have made them choose sides. And I shouldn't have taken my family from you when you needed them the most."

Hunter leaned against the desk, arms crossed, his expression unreadable. Then he sighed. "I got everything I deserved, Marlee."

Silence stretched between them, heavy with unspoken regrets.

Hunter's expression darkened, and he toyed with a paperweight on his desk. "Out of curiosity, were your parents ever bothered by Ben's dealer?"

Marlee blinked. "No. Why? I thought you said you paid his debt."

Hunter shook his head. "I gave him the money to pay it, but Ben bought more drugs instead. He owed a lot of money. Someone came looking for it once after he died. I thought the guy was going to kill me."

Her heart skipped a beat. "Who?"

"I don't know," Hunter admitted. "He was just the heavy. I never met the actual dealer. But I got a message saying someone had to pay up. And when I never heard from him again, I assumed someone had."

An icy dread settled in Marlee's stomach. She knew drug lords didn't just go away. They might bide their time and strike at a later, more unsuspecting moment, but they always got their due, whether in cash, blackmail or even flesh. If Ben had been in debt to dangerous people, they would come calling someday.

She needed to warn her parents. But for the moment, looking at Hunter and seeing the concern etched into his features, that warning would have to wait another day.

Marlee put her tea on the side table. "I'm sorry you were put in a position to be threatened for Ben's choices. No one should have to pay someone else's debts. Ever." Marlee felt an anger well up in her over her brother's problem. It was the first time since he died she was mad at him instead of being mad at Hunter.

But then, wasn't that what she had been doing for eight years? Making Hunter pay for Ben's addiction.

"Actually, I don't agree," Hunter said, standing and joining her on the couch. He bent a leg to face her, and the intensity in those eyes told her to brace herself.

Marlee wondered what else he would say to her tonight.

She asked, "Don't agree about what? You think someone should pay someone else's debt? Sorry, but that's not a world I would want to live in."

"You already do, Marlee. Jesus has paid your debts… He paid for them all, free and clear."

"Oh no, here we go again." Marlee moved to stand. "Please, Hunter. I don't want to talk about God. My days of following blindly are over."

"Good. Because God wants your eyes wide-open. He doesn't want you to miss a thing, especially His love for you. I won't say anything else but this—when I finally realized what God's love looked like, I began seeing evidence of it everywhere in my life. The blinders came off even more when I accepted His love. It's like a light switch turned on, and I could barely catch my breath. The Creator of the Universe loved me. *Me!* Regardless of anything I had done, He still loved me. I realized that all those women I chased over the years had been my way of chasing love. I was lost. I was blind. But not anymore. Now, I'm loved fully, and I don't have to chase any more women for it. In fact, God won't let me."

"Are you telling me this because I kissed you?"

His eyes widened, and he shook his head. "No. You were happy to be alive. I didn't think anything of it."

Marlee released a breath, ready to state her piece. "I'm not talking about today. I'm talking about the night I went to see you after Ben died. The night you called me a kid…right after I kissed you on the cheek."

"Oh… I'm really sorry about the kid thing." Hunter's cheeks reddened. "And don't take this personally, but all I could hear was Ben yelling at me in my head. *Get away from my sister!*" Hunter chuckled. "I once told him you were pretty, and he decked me. He knew me so well and knew I would have hurt you."

Now Marlee felt her cheeks scorch. Hunter thought she was pretty. "Well, thank you for that compliment. If I had known that back then, you never would have gotten rid of me. I fancied myself in love with you."

Hunter tilted his head. "You did? Wow, I had no idea."

Awkward silence stretched between them, and Marlee wondered when she would learn her lesson about sharing too much of herself.

"Yeah, well, it was a long time ago. And like you said, I *was* a kid."

Hunter shook his head. "No, you're not letting me off that easy. Just give me a second to process this. Because all I can see is that all those years I was chasing love, and now you're telling me it was right in front of me the whole time? I'm sorry I made you feel so small. You deserved so much better. Ben was right to keep me away from you."

Marlee frowned but ended the conversation while she was ahead. She stood, yawning. "Well, good night, Hunter. I need to sleep and get back to figuring out the connection between these murders in the morning. And how Nancy Sue fits into all of them. I'll figure it out. Promise." She walked by him, but if he said good night, she hadn't heard it.

Hunter sat at his desk, staring at the darkened screen of his laptop, unable to focus. Marlee's words still echoed in his mind.

She had been in love with him.

All those years, he had thought she only tolerated him because she wanted to follow Ben around. He never once imagined she had felt anything deeper than friendship for him. Even that night she'd kissed him, he hadn't seen it as anything but her fear and grief, just like today when she came off the ledge. And yet, tonight, she had admitted it so openly, as if the truth was the most obvious thing in the world. As if it didn't shake the foundation of everything he'd thought he knew about their past.

He exhaled sharply and ran a hand over his face. Just as he reached for the lamp to turn it off, a bloodcurdling scream split the silence.

Marlee.

Hunter's heart slammed into his ribs as he bolted out of his chair and tore down the hall. He skidded to a stop at her bedroom doorway, his pulse hammering as he took in the scene.

Marlee stood frozen against the wall on the far side of the bed, her wide eyes locked on the writhing form of a rattlesnake coiled on her top sheet. The serpent's tail rattled violently, poised to strike.

It had been under her covers?

"Hunter!" Marlee's voice was barely more than a whisper, but the fear in it made his stomach clench.

"Don't move," he said, his tone calm but firm. He could see the way the snake's head tracked her every breath, every minute shift of her body. One wrong move, and it would strike.

From the second guest room, Gustav barked frantically, sensing his handler's distress. The dog's claws scraped against the door as he tried to break free, but Hunter didn't dare let him charge in. One bite from a rattler and it would be over for him.

Marlee's hands trembled where they scratched at the wall behind her. "How did it get in here?"

Hunter didn't answer. He had a good idea, and it made his blood run cold. Someone had been in here and put it there. Someone had tried to kill her.

But right now, the how didn't matter. Right now, he had to get her out of this alive.

He needed to redirect the snake's attention. He glanced at the nightstand, spotting Marlee's gun. It was close to the bed, but not within reach. He had to be precise.

"Marlee," he said, voice steady. "On my count, I need you to stay completely still. The second I tell you to move, you run straight to me, understand?"

Her eyes met his, desperate and trusting. She gave a tiny nod.

He shifted his stance, calculating the timing. If he missed, there would be no second chance.

"One…two…three!"

Hunter lunged forward, grabbing the gun in one swift motion. The snake sensed the movement and struck, its fangs slicing through empty air as Marlee bolted across the room.

The shot rang out a split second later. The rattlesnake's body coiled violently before it slumped onto the bed, lifeless.

Marlee collided with his chest, her body trembling as he wrapped his arms around her. He held her tightly, feeling the way her heart pounded against his.

"You're okay," he murmured, his hand stroking her back. "I've got you."

Tears wet his shirt as she pressed her face into his shoulder. He pulled back just enough to tilt her chin up, his thumb brushing away the moisture on her cheeks.

She looked up at him, eyes shining with something raw and vulnerable. "I kept thinking it was going to bite me and wondered if you had a bite kit. And if you didn't, how long would it take before I would die?"

"Definitely have a kit, especially with horses. You're safe," he assured her.

"Because of you. That's twice today that you came to my rescue."

"I promised Ben I'd always protect you."

Something passed between them, an unspoken acknowledgment of everything they had been through, everything they had yet to say. Hunter's gaze flicked to her lips, and for the first time, he didn't fight it. He bent his head, pressing a slow, soft kiss to the corner of her mouth, tasting the salt of her tears.

Marlee let out a shaky breath. "I meant what I said earlier. About loving you back then."

Hunter swallowed hard, searching her face for any trace of uncertainty. But all he saw was the truth.

His hand slid to the back of her neck, his resolve weakening as he brought his mouth to hers. The kiss was deep, unhurried—an unraveling of years of pain and longing. She melted into him, her fingers curling into his shirt as if afraid he might disappear.

But he wouldn't. He couldn't. Not anymore.

Then, as quickly as the moment consumed him, reality

crashed down. Hunter pulled away, chest heaving. He had vowed to wait, to trust that God would open the right door in His time. And as much as he wanted to keep kissing her, he knew Marlee Price would never be more than a friend to him. He wouldn't risk hurting her and didn't trust himself not to. As he had told her, Ben was right in telling him to stay away from her.

And he would.

Marlee searched his face, confusion flickering in her eyes. "Hunter?"

He exhaled slowly, pressing his forehead to hers. "I'm honored…"

"But?" She slipped from his arms.

"But this can't happen between us. It never can. I won't hurt you." He walked to the snake and scooped it up in the sheets. "Right now, I need to figure out how this snake got into your bed."

Her face paled but she recovered quickly as she glanced at the sheets. "You think someone put it there?"

"I don't think," he said grimly. "I know."

A chill crept down his spine as he looked around the room, his instincts on high alert. The doors had been locked. The windows shut. Marlee's perimeter traps were all over his property. Yet someone got in. And that meant they weren't just dealing with a killer.

They were dealing with someone who was always watching.

And now, that person had made their move.

TWELVE

At base camp the next morning, Marlee swiped her brow with her forearm, a map spread across the folding table before her. The warm desert air carried the scents of sage and dust as she traced her fingers along the completed search areas marked with Xs. Something about the placement of Nancy Sue's toy nagged at her. It felt too deliberate, too perfect. And it was leading them to search east.

As she studied the layout of the park, she shifted her focus to the west, to the farthest point from where the toy had been found. Her gut told her the kidnapper was leading them in the wrong direction to stop them from finding the real direction the child was, to keep them from searching in an area where they weren't supposed to look.

Charlie approached, coffee in hand, her sharp eyes scanning Marlee's face. "You seem deep in thought. What's on your mind?"

Marlee hesitated before answering. She didn't want to voice her theory just yet. Instead, she asked, pointing at the right-hand corner, "What's on the other side of this plateau?"

The park ranger glanced at the map and shrugged. "Nothing much. A few horse ranches, some private land. Why?"

Marlee simply shook her head. "Just making sure we're covering all possible areas."

Charlie studied her for a moment, then smirked. "I doubt anyone hiked a child over that plateau. It's pretty steep. No way would that be possible. No, we're right where we're supposed to be. Hunter's team knows what they're doing."

Marlee dropped her gaze to the map without agreeing or disagreeing about Hunter's wisdom. After last night, she was questioning the reasons he did anything…like push her away at every turn. She also questioned her willingness to let him get so close. The man had told her he would hurt her. She needed to take him at his word and keep her guard up. It had taken her a long time to heal her heart the last time. She wouldn't risk it again.

"I see I hit a nerve. What's going on with you two? You've been short with him all morning."

Marlee tensed, focusing on the map as if it held all the answers when it was all a blur to her at the moment. "It's nothing."

"That nothing wouldn't have anything to do with the way he sprinted up those hills yesterday, looking like a man who'd jump into the fire for his best friend?"

Marlee glanced up, her chest tightening. "My brother was his best friend. Not me."

"Well, you seem pretty important to him, too. He was as white as a sheet when those guns starting going off. Didn't even hesitate. Are you sure he doesn't care for you, too?"

"Just as his friend's little sister."

Charlie tilted her head. "So he thinks of you as family."

Marlee swallowed hard, and a moment of guilt sucked the air out of her lungs. When Hunter had lost his best friend and needed her family the most, they weren't there for him…because of her. She had heard he'd bought Ben the drugs that killed him, and she went right to her parents to tell them. Knowing what she knew now, that Ben was in debt, Marlee felt like a tattletale.

She tried to remember who had told her about what Hunter had done back then but came up empty. Someone at the school, but that was all she remembered. And it wasn't like Hunter denied it. Hunter paid for those drugs and Ben died. Marlee frowned, looking across the base camp at him. She folded her arms on the table, realizing the dangerous line she'd crossed last night. "Yeah, he thinks of me as family. That's all. That's all it can be."

Charlie took a sip of her coffee and eyed Marlee suspiciously. "You kissed him, didn't you?"

Marlee let out a humorless laugh. "Is it that obvious? It won't happen again. And in my defense, someone put a rattler in my bed last night, but Hunter shot it dead."

Charlie's eyes widened. "Wait—what? Two attempts on your life in one day? Who have you upset? Is it that Clint Jackson? I looked him up. He's bad news."

"In my line of work, the list is endless. But right now, yes, Clint Jackson, a Houston drug lord, is gunning for me and Gustav."

Charlie smiled and downed the last of her coffee. "And Hunter came to the rescue again. I'd kiss someone for rescuing me, too. Especially someone as cute as him."

Marlee pressed a smile back, dropping her attention back to the map. "It was only because I had just faced impending death. That's all."

"Did he kiss you back?"

Marlee's throat dried as she looked past Charlie, watching Hunter as he talked with his team. Her mind replayed the moment from the night before—the way his arms had tightened around her, the way his lips had lingered on hers as if he couldn't bear to let go.

"Yeah, he kissed me back," she admitted quietly.

Charlie shook her head. "Marlee, the way he watches you…

When those gunshots rang out yesterday, he ran into danger for you. He wasn't just being protective. He looked like a man afraid of losing the woman he—" She stopped short. "Well, let's just say he would give his life for you. Not because of your brother. Because of you."

Marlee blinked, stunned by Charlie's words. She wanted to believe them, but doubt clouded her heart. Hunter had always held himself back from her, always let Ben dictate his relationship with her. That hadn't changed, even long after Ben's death.

Charlie gave her a knowing smile before stepping away. "Think about it."

Marlee barely had time to process before Hunter approached, his usual intensity shadowing his features. "We've got a new search area," he said, pointing at the map. "The team's moving out soon."

Marlee's mind was still tangled in Charlie's words, but she forced herself to focus. "I think we're looking in the wrong place." She pointed to the opposite side of the map. "I think the kidnapper planted the toy to keep us searching here. But what if the real location is on the other side of this plateau?"

Hunter frowned. "You want to check it out?"

She nodded. "I'll go myself and meet up with you all later."

"No way. That's not how we work."

"I'll take Charlie with me. As a ranger here, she knows the entire lay of the land."

A muscle ticked in Hunter's jaw. Before he could argue, Michael called out, "Hunter, you ready?"

Marlee watched as conflict crossed his face. She knew the moment he realized he had to make a choice—go with Michael and the team or follow her.

Charlie's words echoed in Marlee's mind as she held Hunter's gaze. Whether or not he admitted it, he would give his life for her. The question was…why?

And was she willing to let him?

Marlee saw his hesitation, the war within him. She folded the map and stuck it in her backpack. "Go with your team. Charlie will come with me."

Hunter lowered his voice. "After everything that happened yesterday—"

Charlie cut in, approaching them. "We'll be fine. I need to make my rounds, anyway."

"I'm not really on board with this," Hunter said, but Marlee had made up her mind. With clear reluctance, he nodded. Marlee watched him lead Libby down the opposite path, then took Gustav and turned toward Charlie's ranger SUV.

As they drove away from the team, Marlee caught Charlie smiling while looking in the rearview mirror.

"He likes you," she teased in a singsong voice.

But Marlee was done with the park ranger's matchmaking antics. She faced forward to the expansive vista before her and focused on finding a little girl somewhere out there.

Hunter moved through the rugged terrain with his team, his boots crunching against the dry dirt. The morning sun had fully risen, casting long shadows through the canyon. His thoughts, however, weren't on the search at hand. They were still tangled up in the night before—Marlee's kiss, the way she had clung to him after the rattlesnake incident, the way he had almost let himself believe for one reckless moment that they could be something more.

But they couldn't. He had made his choices, drawn his lines. He would wait for God. Hunter would not open the door to dating again until God readied him for someone. Hunter would not take the chance of hurting another person, even if that meant never dating again.

Michael's voice pulled him from his thoughts. "Hunter, we need to talk."

Hunter glanced at his friend and nodded, falling into step beside him as the rest of the team moved ahead. "What's on your mind?"

Michael's expression was hard to read, but his tone was pointed. "You and Marlee."

Hunter paused mid-step. "There is no 'me and Marlee.'"

Michael scoffed. "Right. That's why you've been acting like a man about to step off a cliff. I know you, Hunter. You're getting too close, and it's a mistake."

Hunter exhaled sharply. "Nothing is happening. And even if it was, what's it to you?"

Michael's jaw tightened. "Because I've seen you like this before. With Donna. And we both know how that turned out. Your relationships never end well. Then I watch you walk around with all this guilt."

A memory of that time surfaced, and so did the pain of failure. He turned fully to Michael. "That was different. I messed that relationship up. I…wanted it to work so much, I pushed her away and made her run. It was all my fault."

Michael crossed his arms. "That's what I'm talking about. You'll take the blame when Marlee drops you, too. She's DEA, Hunter. She's not staying here. You get caught up in this, and you're gonna be the one left behind again."

Hunter let out a bitter laugh. "Donna had every right to run. But you don't have to worry about me and Marlee. I'm not opening that door. But Marlee is helping with this investigation, and you need to accept that. You really want to help? Find out what Donna was facing. I found mail at her place. She was in some kind of legal battle."

Michael frowned. "Legal battle over what?"

Hunter shook his head. "I don't know. But whatever it was, she kept it quiet. And then there's this mess in the canyon. She wasn't here for a news story. She was into something bigger."

Michael considered that, then sighed. "So what do you think was really going on?"

Hunter ran a hand over his jaw. "I don't know yet. But I know that meth lab was too small. When I heard 'drug operation,' I expected a massive network, not just a busted-up trailer. That place was not story worthy. And we found it way too easy. Donna would have, too, if that's what she was here for." Hunter shook his head. "There's more to it all. And it got her killed."

The team walked on, spreading out to cover more land. As Hunter and Michael followed a branch-off trail, something dark in a bush caught Hunter's attention.

"Hold up. I want to see what this is," he said, leading Libby to a cactus plant. With gloves, he removed a piece of black fabric from the prickers. Spreading it wide, he noticed a white brand on one corner.

"'LV,'" he read aloud, recognizing the initials and looking down the trail and at the surrounding area to get his bearings. "We're facing west, right?"

Michael checked his compass. "Due west, yup. What are you thinking?"

"I'm wondering why Lone Vida Ranch would have one of their handkerchiefs in the middle of the canyon."

Michael shrugged. "The ranch is on the outskirts of the park. Some ranch hand left it on a post and a good wind could have carried it here. That'd be my guess."

"Over the plateau? I would think it would have caught on something on the other side before making it up and over to settle here." He wondered if he was grasping at straws when he said, "Perhaps someone from the ranch is involved in the kidnapping, and they *did* carry Nancy Sue over that plateau. Marlee thought someone's been feeding us breadcrumbs to keep us away from the actual operation, and to keep us on this side of the park. But what if Nancy Sue's been dropping these things to help us find her? What if these aren't breadcrumbs leading us astray but were dropped along the way over that plateau, and they *did* come this way?"

Michael squinted into the western sun. "That's a tough trek for a child. I think the handkerchief is another crumb, leading us astray. I say we stay east. I don't think a young child would know enough to drop things, nor get the chance to."

"Why not? She saw her mother murdered. Maybe even the undercover cop. She knows she's in danger." A sudden, cold realization swept over Hunter. "And now Marlee's heading straight into the area where that danger might be waiting."

Michael said, "She's a federal agent, Hunter. She can take care of herself. It's time you saw her for what she is—a trained professional. Not someone who needs you to save her."

Hunter stared at him. "I respect that she's capable, but that doesn't mean she shouldn't have backup."

Michael's voice took on a harder edge. "This isn't about providing her backup. This is about you getting distracted when you need to focus on this case."

Hunter gritted his teeth. Michael had never said these things to him. But he was wrong.

"As I have told you, Marlee is a friend, and that is all she will ever be. Now I'm heading back to base camp to grab my truck. I'm driving over to the other side, but I want this trail over the plateau searched by the team. Keep me posted with anything else you find. Nancy Sue is proving to be a smart kid. She has her wits about her, and that tells me she's alive and well. But she's still in serious trouble...and so is Marlee, if she's caught unawares."

Michael sighed and called to Hunter's retreating back, "You're making a mistake. Friends don't let friends get dumped on. And that's exactly what she'll do. Just like the last time."

Hunter stopped cold and turned back to his friend, giving him a steady look. "No. Friends don't let friends walk into danger alone. And Marlee is my friend, too, Michael. I need you to understand that."

Without another word, he turned and headed back the way they had come. He had to find Marlee before it was too late.

THIRTEEN

Marlee gripped the edge of her seat as Charlie navigated off-road over uneven dirt trails, leading them deep into the westernmost side of the park. The farther they drove, the more desolate the landscape became. Sparse vegetation and jagged rock formations stretched endlessly beneath the clear early-evening sky, creating an eerie stillness.

Charlie pulled the SUV to a stop near a cluster of towering sandstone cliffs. She unbuckled her seat belt and gestured outward. "This is no-man's-land."

Marlee scanned the area. It was barren, untouched by frequent hikers or casual campers. The ground was uneven, riddled with loose gravel and deep crevices. Towering rock formations created a labyrinth of winding passages and shadowy alcoves.

"Nancy Sue couldn't have been brought all the way out here," Charlie continued. "Not without leaving some kind of trace. There are no roads that lead this far in. Most of these paths are impassable by vehicle. And water is pretty much nonexistent."

Marlee nodded, but a nagging feeling told her to search, anyway. She stepped out of the SUV and let her boots sink into the soft, shifting sand. Gustav padded beside her, his ears alert and nose twitching. She crouched down, brushing her fingertips across the surface.

Then she saw a single footprint, partially eroded by the wind.

Her pulse quickened. “Charlie, look at this.”

The ranger knelt beside her, examining the impression. “It could be anything. A stray hiker, maybe. And who knows when that might’ve been? If there were more prints at one time, they’ve been erased.”

Marlee stood, scanning the terrain. “It’s worth checking out.”

Charlie exhaled but nodded. “All right, but be careful. This place is a maze. I don’t want to lose you. I’ll keep watch at this location. Call out if you need me.”

Marlee agreed with the ranger keeping watch and made her way toward a narrow path, cutting between two massive rock formations. The farther she walked, the tighter the passage became. The towering walls pressed in, forcing Marlee to shift sideways to squeeze through. She moved cautiously, her fingers brushing against the cool stone for balance.

“You still hear me?” she called out.

“Yeah! But barely!” Charlie’s voice echoed back. “Don’t go much farther. I’m not small like you. I’ll get stuck if I have to go in after you.”

Marlee continued forward, Gustav staying close behind in single file. The canyon twisted in unpredictable turns, some openings barely wide enough for her shoulders. Sunlight struggled to reach the deeper crevices, casting long, ominous shadows along the rock walls.

She turned another sharp corner and paused, listening. “Charlie?”

Silence.

Her chest tightened. “Charlie? Can you hear me?”

Her voice bounced off the walls in an endless loop, but no reply came. She swallowed hard and turned to retrace her steps, but the path had twisted so much she wasn't sure which way was back. Gustav let out a low whimper, sensing her hesitation.

Panic threatened to set in, but she forced herself to stay calm. She had navigated worse situations. She just needed to…

The sudden shift of light ahead made her freeze.

Two men stepped from the shadows, rifles raised.

Marlee's heart slammed against her ribs. She reached for her weapon, but before she could react, one of them turned his rifle toward Gustav.

"Don't," the man warned with an accent.

Marlee's breath caught. The cold handle of her own gun suddenly felt useless in her hands. She couldn't risk Gustav's life.

Slowly, she lifted her hands in surrender and let her weapon drop to the ground.

"Smart choice, amiga," the second man muttered, stepping closer. "Now, you're coming with us."

Her pulse pounded, but she kept her expression unreadable. She wasn't going down without a fight. But she would need to find the right moment to make her move.

The men led Marlee at gunpoint, one ahead and one behind. Gustav padded at her side, his eyes flicking between the armed men and his handler. He was waiting for her command, but Marlee didn't dare risk it yet.

As they climbed a small hill, she caught sight of what lay beyond, and her stomach lurched.

A full-scale drug operation.

This was so much bigger than the run-down trailer that kid had led them to. This was the nucleus of the empire. Tucked inside the rocks and protected from view by the slot canyons that no vehicle could get into—though judging by the trucks, they had a secret way in somehow. This was the place she had been looking for.

Dozens of people moved around a portable village—makeshift tents, storage containers and camouflaged vehicles scattered across the area. Smoke curled from fires where people cooked food, and large barrels sat filled with unknown chemicals. Marlee's breath hitched as she spotted workers—many appearing to be migrant laborers—engaged in various tasks. Some sorted supplies, while others managed large plastic containers filled with what she assumed were illicit substances. Judging by Gustav's agitation, he smelled it all.

Then her gaze landed on a small figure kneeling by a basin of water.

A little girl washing clothes.

Marlee's heart clenched as the girl lifted her head, revealing familiar hazel eyes.

Nancy Sue.

A sharp breath escaped Marlee's lips. She had suspected it, but seeing the child here, in the middle of this nightmare, made it real. Her resemblance to Hunter was undeniable—those same piercing hazel eyes, the same determined expression. She looked just like Hunter.

Marlee's first instinct was to call out, to reach for the child, but she bit back the urge. She couldn't scare her. She had to earn her trust.

Nancy Sue's gaze met hers. The girl's expression turned wary. Before Marlee could offer a reassuring smile, Nancy Sue turned and bolted, disappearing between the tents.

Marlee's chest tightened. What had they done to this child to make her so afraid?

Before she could dwell on it, the men pushed her toward a large tent at the center of the village. She forced herself to keep calm. If she played this right, she could break free—with Nancy Sue.

She just needed a plan.

But just as they shoved her inside the flap, one man grabbed Gustav's collar, causing the dog to bark aggressively. The other man blocked Marlee from going after her dog, and when she tried to push past him, he raised his rifle and brought it down on her head.

Lights out.

Hunter gripped the steering wheel tightly as his truck rumbled over the rugged dirt path. The vast, empty expanse of the westernmost part of the park stretched before him, rocky formations casting long shadows under the late-afternoon sun. The nagging feeling in his gut had grown stronger with every passing mile. Something wasn't right.

Libby stirred in her cage in the truck bed, letting out a low whine. She sensed his tension.

He slowed the vehicle, scanning the terrain for any sign of Charlie's park ranger SUV, but the area Marlee had pointed out on the map was completely empty. No tire tracks, no sign that a vehicle had passed through recently. He frowned in frustration.

Reaching for his radio, he switched to the sheriff's channel. "Sheriff Hawkins, you got a copy?"

Static crackled before a response came through. "Yeah, Shelton. What's going on?"

"I'm out on the west side, where Marlee planned to check out a lead. I don't see her or Charlie's vehicle anywhere. Any word from either of them?"

Hawkins sighed. "Not since they left the search. But listen, we just got the results from the hair sample."

Hunter sat up straighter. "And?"

"It's her, Hunter. The DNA is a match for Nancy Sue. Her mother had her DNA put into a child-find system in case she ever went missing. It's hers."

Hunter's chest constricted. He had already suspected it, but hearing the confirmation made it real.

"Poor child," he murmured, more to himself than to Hawkins. "She's got to be terrified. I think she's been dropping items along the path that the kidnapper took her on. She's a smart kid."

"Her father's been raising his voice over here, demanding more action. He's furious we haven't found her yet. Or at least tracked down a lead. Anything you can tell me I can relay to him?"

Hunter swallowed hard. He didn't blame the man. If she were his child…

A thought struck him hard. *What if she is mine?* The possibility that had been lurking in the back of his mind suddenly surged to the forefront.

Was Nancy Sue his child?

No. Donna's journal stated clearly who the father was. Hunter shook the thought away. This wasn't the time to focus on that. He had to rescue her and bring her home…to her father.

"Not yet, but we're looking constantly," Hunter said, twisting his hands tightly on the wheel again. "Let me know if you get anything new."

"Will do." Hawkins hesitated. "And Hunter—Marlee's a federal agent. She knows what she's doing. Try not to let your personal feelings cloud your judgment."

Hunter clenched his jaw. That was the second time today someone had told him to let Marlee handle herself. Maybe they were right. Maybe he needed to question his need to protect her.

But even as he considered it, something in his gut told him Marlee was in danger.

He pressed his foot harder on the gas, dust kicking up around his truck. As he rounded a bend, something caught his eye—a thin column of smoke rising into the sky in the distance.

Someone had a fire going.

Campers?

His pulse quickened. Maybe they'd seen Marlee.

Hunter didn't hesitate. He turned the wheel toward the smoke and pressed forward, praying this was a lead to find her.

The terrain grew rougher, the path narrowing between rocky outcroppings. He slowed down, scanning his surroundings. Every nerve in his body was on high alert. He'd been in enough dangerous situations to recognize when he was walking into one.

Then, a flicker of movement.

Hunter barely had time to react before gunfire erupted.

Bullets slammed into the side of his truck, shattering the side mirror and punching through the metal frame. Hunter ducked, yanking the wheel hard to the right. The truck fishtailed on the uneven terrain, kicking up a cloud of dust and gravel.

Libby barked furiously from her kennel, her snarls a mix of rage and frustration.

Hunter reached for his sidearm, but before he could draw it, another bullet took out a front tire. The truck lurched violently, throwing him forward as the vehicle skidded out of control. The steering wheel wrenched from his grip, and he braced for impact as the truck slammed into a rocky embankment.

The world spun.

Dazed, Hunter struggled to get his bearings. Blood trickled

down his forehead from where he'd hit the steering wheel. His vision blurred, but he forced himself to move. He had to fight.

The driver's side door was yanked open, and rough hands grabbed him, dragging him out of the cab before he could resist. His gun was ripped from its holster. A man dressed in black shoved him onto his knees in the dirt.

Hunter's head throbbed, but he still lifted his gaze, taking stock of his captors.

Five men. Armed. Militant. Their eyes held a ruthless intent while their faces were partially covered with bandannas.

The same black bandanna he had found at the search site with the Lone Vida brand.

One of them, a tall man with a scar below his left eye, stepped forward and cracked Hunter across the face with the butt of his rifle. Pain exploded across his jaw, and he nearly toppled over.

"You looking for the woman?" the man demanded. His accent was thick, but his words were clear.

Hunter spat blood into the dirt and lifted his chin defiantly. "What woman?"

The man smirked. "The one who's been sniffing around where she doesn't belong." He nodded to another man, who lifted a radio and spoke in rapid Spanish.

Hunter's stomach dropped. They had Marlee.

Before he could react, the man slammed the rifle into Hunter's ribs. White-hot pain shot through his right side, tearing the stitches, and he gritted his teeth to keep from crying out.

Behind him, Libby barked frantically, her body straining against the kennel door. He could hear her claws scraping against the metal, her desperate attempts to get to him. But she was trapped, helpless to stop what was happening.

"Get him up," the leader ordered.

Two men grabbed Hunter's arms and hauled him to his

feet. He struggled, but a hard punch to his stomach stole his breath, leaving him doubled over in pain.

They forced him forward, shoving him toward a hill of rocks that lined a dirt path. Each step sent sharp pain lancing through his ribs, but he refused to show weakness. They pushed him up and over and down into the earth. Hunter knew he would never be found here.

As they crested the last hill, Hunter's breath hitched at the sight below.

A full-blown encampment with armed guards posted at key points, their rifles slung across their chests. He sought ways to escape while he had the high vantage point.

Then his gaze caught on a small girl, no older than five, standing near a fire pit. She clutched a piece of cloth in her tiny hands, staring at him with wide, familiar hazel eyes.

Hunter's breath caught in his throat.

Nancy Sue.

The child's expression was filled with a deep sadness… and fear. She held a silent understanding that she knew he was scared, too. Before Hunter could process it, a sharp blow to the back of his head sent him crashing to the ground. Darkness swallowed him whole.

FOURTEEN

Marlee's hands ached from scrubbing clothes against the washboard, but she didn't stop. The other women around her worked in silence, their heads down, moving mechanically, as though afraid to do anything outside of their given tasks. None of them spoke English, and even if they did, Marlee doubted they would risk conversation under the watchful eyes of the armed guards stationed around the work area. The heavy atmosphere of sweat, fear and exhaustion pressed down on her like an iron weight.

She kept her gaze moving, scanning the camp in search of Nancy Sue. But the child was nowhere to be seen. It had been twenty-four hours since Marlee saw her run off in fright. Marlee's heart ached at the thought of what the little girl must be going through, trapped in this place.

A sudden commotion drew the attention of the two guards watching the women. Two of the workers were arguing, their voices raised. One of them shoved the other, and just like that, the guards stormed over, momentarily distracted. Marlee seized the opportunity. Slipping away from the group, she darted behind a stack of supply crates and ducked low, making sure she wasn't seen. Then she crept toward a row of tents on the outskirts of the camp.

She reached the first tent and slipped inside. It was dark,

and the musty scents of sweat and mildew permeated the space. The sound of a moan had her nearly running out—until she spotted a man lying on a bedroll in the corner.

Marlee approached him slowly, gasping at the sight of the man. He'd been beaten to a bloody pulp. He was nearly unrecognizable—except for the matted blond curls.

Hunter.

She rushed to his side, kneeling beside him. His face was pale, a deep gash on his forehead, his shirt stained with blood. She pressed a hand to his forehead—he was burning up.

Panic surged through her. He needed medical attention. If his injuries became infected, he could die. He could have internal bleeding she couldn't see. She lifted his shirt to see dark bruising around his ribs.

Before she could think of her next move, the tent flap rustled. Marlee whirled, her muscles coiling in anticipation of a fight—only to freeze when she saw the small figure standing at the entrance.

Nancy Sue.

The little girl clutched a small ice block in her hands with a black rag. Her hazel eyes flickered from Marlee to Hunter, uncertainty and fear warring in her expression. Then, without a word, she stepped forward and knelt on the opposite side of Hunter and placed the ice against his forehead.

Marlee's heart squeezed at the simple act of kindness. She watched as the little girl carefully dabbed at Hunter's wound, her tiny hands trembling.

Swallowing the lump in her throat, Marlee softened her voice. "Hey, sweetheart. My name's Marlee. Thank you for bringing ice. That was so nice of you."

Nancy Sue hesitated before giving a small nod.

Marlee smiled, keeping her tone gentle. "You're doing a great job helping Hunter."

Nancy Sue didn't reply, but she didn't run, either. That was something.

Marlee took a deep breath. "Are you okay? Are they hurting you?"

Nancy Sue lowered her gaze, her tiny fingers clutching the edge of her ragged dress. After a long pause, she whispered, "They killed my mommy, and now they make me work."

Marlee's stomach twisted. This poor child had been taken, forced into labor. Marlee had to get her out of here.

"I know your mommy," Marlee said carefully.

Tears welled in Nancy Sue's eyes. "Mommy's gone."

Marlee's chest ached. She reached out slowly, brushing a few strands of hair from Nancy Sue's face. "I'm so sorry, sweetheart."

The little girl sniffled. "Mommy and Daddy were fighting."

Marlee's breath caught. "Fighting about what?"

Nancy Sue looked down at Hunter, then back up at Marlee. Her voice was barely above a whisper. "Me."

Marlee's heart pounded as she pondered the couple's relationship since they broke up. Perhaps the legal battle had been over custody of Nancy Sue.

But if Nancy Sue turned out not to be Leon's biological child, would he have killed Donna…or, more likely, had her killed by someone in this drug ring? A hired assassin. But why allow his child to live in this encampment as slave labor?

Maybe Leon didn't want Nancy Sue anymore, now that he knew he wasn't the father…

Before she could ask Nancy Sue any more questions, a heavy boot stomped outside. The tent flap flew open, and a guard loomed in the entrance, his glare locking onto Marlee.

She rose quickly, positioning herself between him and Nancy Sue. "He needs help," she said, jerking her chin toward Hunter. "If you don't take care of him, he'll die. People are looking for him. It would benefit you to keep him alive. Please, I can help him. Both of us can." Marlee nodded toward Nancy Sue.

The guard scowled but didn't argue. Instead, he grabbed Marlee's arm roughly and yanked her toward the exit.

Marlee shot one last look at Nancy Sue. The little girl's eyes were wide with fear, but she didn't run this time.

Marlee sent her a reassuring smile before being dragged toward the exit.

"Please!" Nancy Sue shouted. "I need help."

The guard stopped, still scowling. He dropped Marlee's arm. "Twenty-four hours. Then it's back to work with the washing."

"I understand," Marlee said, taking a step back away from the foul-smelling guard. He left them, shouting orders at people outside. As his voice grew distant, Marlee expelled a deep breath and turned back to Nancy Sue and Hunter.

Hunter's fevered eyes opened, and he and the child stared at her with the same intensity, so identical, there was no way they weren't father and daughter.

Hunter drifted between consciousness and darkness, his body burning and chilled at once. He felt weightless, untethered, as if he were floating. But in the moments of clarity, he was aware of gentle hands pressing something cool against his forehead. A voice—soft, soothing—murmured words he couldn't quite grasp, but they wrapped around him like a lifeline, keeping him from slipping completely into oblivion.

He forced his eyes open, blinking against the dim light filtering into the tent. The fever still made his vision hazy, but he recognized Marlee immediately. She knelt beside him, concern tightening her expression as she pressed a damp cloth to his brow. Relief flooded through him at finding her alive. He tried to move his hand to touch her but had no strength. She was so beautiful, and he nearly told her so.

"You're awake," she breathed in relief. "How do you feel?"

Hunter tried to speak, but his throat was dry and raw. He swallowed, grimacing at the effort. "Like I got run over," he rasped.

Marlee let out a small, humorless chuckle. "Close enough." She reached for a wooden bowl and lifted it to his lips. "Drink."

He sipped, the warm broth sliding down his throat and easing some of the discomfort. As he adjusted to his surroundings, his gaze flickered to the small figure hovering beside Marlee.

A little girl watching him cautiously.

His fevered mind struggled to piece things together, but the realization came crashing down like a landslide.

Nancy Sue.

She was right here, within arm's reach. She wasn't just an image in a case file or a lost child they were searching for. She was real. And more than that, she was staring at him with the same intense gaze he saw in the mirror every morning.

His chest tightened.

"Hi there," he murmured, his voice rough but as gentle as he could make it to not scare her.

Nancy Sue hesitated, but then moved closer, her small hands tightening around the cloth she held. "Are you still sick?" she asked.

Hunter blinked at her innocence, his heart squeezing at the concern in her voice. "A little," he admitted. "But I think I'll be okay."

Nancy Sue nodded, then placed the ice she had been holding on his forehead, just as he'd sensed someone doing before. It had been Nancy Sue caring for him. His heart swelled with a powerful emotion he couldn't place. Instant love? Was that possible?

Marlee smiled at the child, exchanging a look with Hunter that answered his question. Yes, it *was* possible, and it looked like Marlee felt the same way for her.

For a long moment, Hunter just stared at the little girl, memorizing every detail. Her delicate features, the way she worried her bottom lip, how she moved with a quiet gentleness. And that she was here—safe for the moment—made him realize he hadn't failed in saving her…yet.

Marlee's voice was soft when she spoke. "She's been looking after you."

Hunter turned his gaze back to Marlee. "You, too?"

She smirked. "Wouldn't want you dying on my watch."

He wanted to say more, but exhaustion dragged him under. His last sight before his eyes closed again was of Marlee and Nancy Sue sitting beside him, two figures that shouldn't have felt like home—but somehow, they did.

He stirred again during the night. He could hear snoring in the tent next to his, but when he turned the other way, he noticed Marlee sleeping against the pole at the center of the tent. Nancy Sue was curled up in Marlee's arms, also sleeping soundly. Hunter smiled and let sleep take him into the darkness again.

The next time he woke, it was to the sensation of warm fur pressed against his arm. He stirred, his fingers twitching, and felt the familiar weight of a large, sturdy head resting beside him.

Libby.

His loyal K-9 was alive and safe. Relief flooded Hunter, stronger than anything else he had felt in the last hours of hallucinations. Was any of it real? He turned his head slightly and caught sight of Marlee standing at the entrance of the tent.

Nancy Sue was beside her, carefully balancing another bowl of broth in her hands.

Marlee stepped forward and pressed a hand to his forehead, her expression unreadable. "Your fever's broken," she announced, but there was something in her voice that told him she wasn't entirely relieved.

He raised a brow, his voice hoarse. "That a bad thing?"

Marlee sighed. "It means they're going to expect me and Nancy Sue to get back to work."

Hunter scowled. "Then I'll just have to keep being sick."

Marlee rolled her eyes. "Somehow, I don't think they'll buy that for much longer."

Hunter reached for her hand before she could pull away. His grip was weak, but he held on as best he could. "Be careful," he said, his voice low and serious. "Don't take any unnecessary risks. But I want you to get out of here. Don't worry about me. Take Nancy Sue and get out of here."

She squeezed his hand in return. "I'm not leaving without either of you. Or the dogs. They have Gustav in a cage at the outskirts of the camp."

Hunter's throat tightened at the conviction in her tone. He believed her. "Please, Marlee. For me. Get her out."

Marlee sighed, but then begrudgingly nodded in agreement with his plan. For the first time since waking up in this prison camp, Hunter felt a sliver of hope. Even if he died, Marlee and Nancy Sue would be all right.

If he couldn't break out with them, he would make sure they escaped without being killed.

FIFTEEN

The tension in the camp was palpable, but through it all, Marlee had watched Hunter regain his strength. His fever had broken, and the color had returned to his face, though the bruises and cuts still marked his skin. They couldn't afford to wait any longer. Their time for escape was running out.

Marlee sat beside Hunter on the edge of his cot, holding him up as his strength returned.

"You have to move tonight," Hunter said, his hushed voice firm. "They're already talking about separating us. They'll take Nancy Sue and you somewhere else, maybe even to another camp."

Marlee swallowed hard, not liking the idea of leaving him behind. "You'll need to create a diversion for us to get away."

Hunter nodded. "If I break into Gustav's kennel and let him out, he'll be the chaos we need. As soon as you hear Gustav is out, you whistle for him and take Nancy Sue and Libby. Run. Don't look back."

Marlee clenched her fists, her stomach twisting with unease. She looked away, knowing this was the only way, but hating it just the same. Her throat felt thick as she whispered, "I don't want to leave you. I think we should stay together." The honesty in her voice in this critical moment spoke of more than the present.

Hunter reached for her, his hands gentle but firm as he pulled her into an embrace. Marlee rested her forehead on his shoulder, her conflict battling her instinct to hold on to him and stay by his side. It didn't feel right to leave him behind. It didn't feel right to let him go at all.

Because it never was.

Hunter's voice rumbled against her ear. "It has to be this way, Marlee. You know it."

She pulled back slightly, staring up at his bruised face, so full of determination and sacrifice. Slowly, she leaned in, her heart hammering in her chest. She paused just before their lips touched, searching his face for hesitation, for doubt.

There was none.

Hunter closed the gap between them, his lips claiming hers in a deep, lingering kiss that stole the breath from her lungs. Marlee melted into him, gripping his shirt, not wanting to ever let go. It wasn't just a kiss of desperation or fear—it was an unspoken truth between them.

Hunter had always been a part of her family, but he was also a part of her, and she could no longer deny it.

A shuffling sound broke them apart. They turned to see Nancy Sue entering the tent with Libby at her side, a quizzical look in the child's eyes.

"What are you doing?" Nancy Sue asked, tilting her head in curiosity.

Marlee couldn't help but smile, though her face was warm with embarrassment. "Didn't you ever see your mommy and daddy kiss?"

Nancy Sue shook her head. "No. They never did anything like that."

Marlee exchanged a look with Hunter, both of them silently absorbing the meaning of that statement. What kind of relationship had Donna and Leon really had? Was it all a lie?

Hunter knelt to Nancy Sue's level, placing a reassuring hand on her small shoulder. "Sweet girl, I need you to stay with Marlee, okay? No matter what happens, you listen to her and do exactly what she says. Can you do that for me?"

Nancy Sue nodded, her tiny face solemn with understanding. "I promise."

Hunter smiled, brushing a strand of hair from her face. Then he stood and turned back to Marlee. "It's time."

Marlee hesitated, still battling the urge to throw caution at the wind and stay by his side. But Hunter was already walking toward the tent flap, ready to step into the night.

Before he could leave, he reached out and touched a finger to her lips, his voice a low whisper. "We're not done here."

Then he was gone.

Marlee stood frozen for a moment, her fingers brushing over her lips where she could still feel his touch. Her heart ached, but there was no time to linger on it. They had a mission to complete.

Nancy Sue tugged on Marlee's sleeve, her voice barely above a whisper. "What do you want me to do?"

Marlee inhaled deeply, straightening her shoulders. "Get ready to run. Because in just a few minutes, we have to run for our lives. No looking back, okay, sweetie? Just keep running."

Nancy Sue wrapped her arms around Marlee's waist and tipped her head back. "I'm a fast runner. Mommy told me to run, too, and I did. I ran real fast." The child frowned instantly. "But she couldn't run as fast."

Marlee pressed tears away and finger combed Nancy Sue's curls, forcing a smile at the child. "I promise to keep up with you. I won't leave your side."

A shout outside the tent alerted them to move. A commotion broke out almost immediately. The sharp sounds of men shouting and Gustav barking rang out through the camp. Marlee grasped the girl's hand, her pulse pounding in her ears. This was it. Their one and only chance.

Peering outside the tent, Marlee spotted Hunter near the open cage, struggling against three men with guns drawn. She knew the plan—whistle for Gustav and run. But the sight of those rifles aimed at Hunter changed everything. If they shot him now, their plan would be for nothing.

Without hesitation, Marlee commanded, "Gustav, attack!"

The K-9 lunged from the cage, locking his jaws onto one of the men's arms. The guard screamed, tumbling to the ground as he fought against the dog's powerful grip.

Hunter shot her a sharp look of frustration, but in the next breath, he seized the moment to fight back. He tackled the second guard, wrestling for control of the man's weapon. The third man raised his rifle, aiming at Hunter's head just as Hunter gained control of the gun and shot the third man first.

Marlee's breath caught in her throat, but it was time. "Gustav, off! Come!" She whistled, and the dog immediately released his hold and sprinted toward her.

Gunfire erupted behind them. Marlee pushed forward, yanking Nancy Sue along as they sprinted through the camp. Libby followed, with Gustav coming up behind her and reaching their sides.

They reached the slot canyon, its towering rock walls casting deep shadows around them. The narrow passages forced Marlee to twist and squeeze through, the sounds of shouting fading behind them. Adrenaline fueled her, but fear threatened to freeze her limbs. She forced herself to keep going. She couldn't let the trauma hinder her now. Each time became easier, which was good, because Nancy Sue was depending on her to keep up with her. Marlee had made her a promise.

Nancy Sue panted beside her, her small hand tightening around Marlee's. "Are we almost safe?"

"Almost, sweetheart. Just a little farther. Keep running."

Time felt long in the complete darkness, but Marlee remembered the route in and knew she could get them out.

"I'm scared. I can't see," the girl said.

"I'm right beside you. The walls will guide you."

Finally, they pushed through and emerged from the canyon, tumbling out onto their knees. But they had to keep going. The men wouldn't be too far behind.

But would Hunter be?

Headlights bounced off in the distance, causing Marlee's heart to lift with hope. The open landscape stretched before them as they raced for the road. As it neared, Marlee waved frantically at the vehicle.

It was Charlie's SUV.

Relief flooded Marlee. They weren't alone. Help had come. And soon more would be here to help Hunter.

Charlie must have spotted them, because the SUV sped forward. Marlee pushed herself harder, her lungs burning, and soon the vehicle skidded to a stop.

The ranger threw the driver's door open, her face filled with concern. "Marlee! Oh, thank God. We've been looking for you! And you have Nancy Sue! You did it! You found her!"

Marlee barely had time to process the praise. She ushered the dogs into the hatchback of the vehicle, then rushed into the front passenger seat with Nancy Sue on her lap. "We need to go, now! The men won't be far behind. You need to call for help. They have Hunter."

Charlie nodded, shifting into gear. "You're amazing, Marlee. I knew you could do it."

Marlee waited for Charlie to make the call…but she didn't.

Gustav growled and barked aggressively, as though he was tracking drugs.

Marlee's stomach dropped as she realized something was

off. The woman not only didn't make the call, but she also wasn't turning toward headquarters. She was heading west—farther into the wilderness.

"Charlie…where are we going? We need backup!" Marlee reached for the ranger's phone on the console.

Before Marlee touched it, a firm hand clamped over her mouth from behind, yanking her head back to the seat and pressing a damp cloth to her face. Marlee twisted fruitlessly as a sickly sweet scent filled her nostrils. Chloroform.

Her vision blurred. Her muscles weakened. Nancy Sue's distant cry as she was also smothered with the chemical was the last thing Marlee heard before darkness swallowed her whole.

Hunter raced to the canyons. He had finally disposed of the guards and expected more to attack. But just as he entered the stone walls, he realized he wouldn't fit through. He would need to go back the way he had been brought in. Wasting more time.

Frustrated, Hunter slipped back out, expecting to come face to face with more guards. Instead, everyone rushed around, packing up the camp.

Tents were being taken down, supplies gathered, and workers were hurriedly loading up the vehicles. They knew their time was up and law enforcement would be here soon.

Or they knew something Hunter didn't know. Dread coiled in his gut as he turned his attention back to the guards shouting orders.

Hunter ran up to one, grabbing his shirt and demanded, "What's going on?"

The guard let out a sharp laugh, his lip curling in amusement. "You really don't get it, do you?" He spat on the dirt and grinned. "Your woman and her dog are worth a pot of gold. And today's payday."

Hunter's blood ran cold.

Clint Jackson.

The drug cartel had sold Marlee and Gustav to Clint Jackson for the bounty. And Hunter…

Hunter had sent her right into the drug lord's hands.

A roar ripped from his throat, but instead of running, which in his state of physical health wouldn't get him far, Hunter made the only choice he could.

"Take me to her. Sell me as well. I'm hurt now, but I'll heal. I'm an able-bodied male. I'm worth some money, too."

The guard squinted in shock, but then shrugged and removed a black bandana from his coat. "It's your funeral, amigo."

The guard tied on the blindfold, while Hunter prayed that when the bandana came off, he would see Marlee and Nancy Sue again.

In the next second, hands wrapped a rope around his chest, securing his arms to his torso. Then they tied his legs together as if he was a piece of meat packaged up in a butcher shop. Someone pushed him forward, throwing him face down in the dirt. Before he could catch his breath from the pain, he felt his body strain against the ropes as he was picked up and tossed blindly into the back of a truck bed, landing hard like a sack of potatoes. Without bracing for impact, excruciating pain exploded in his ribs, and he nearly vomited. Hunter asked for this, but would he survive it? As bright lights flashed behind the blindfold, he let his body take him under to the pain-free darkness of unconsciousness.

SIXTEEN

Marlee's head pounded as she drifted back into consciousness, her body sluggish and unresponsive. A damp, musty scent filled her nostrils, the air thick with the scents of hay, old wood and something more pungent—oil, maybe. Her arms and ankles throbbed as she struggled against the binds that held her, and when she tried to cry out, a rough fabric gag stifled her voice.

Her eyes fluttered open, adjusting to the dim shafts of bright sunlight slipping through the cracks in a barn's ceiling and walls. The surrounding space was cavernous, but eerily silent. No sound of Nancy Sue's small voice. No soft whimpers from Gustav or Libby.

Panic clawed at her chest. Where were they?

She turned onto her side. Her cheek pressed against the grimy floorboards as she wriggled, testing the tightness of her restraints. If she didn't get out of here, she couldn't help them. Fighting back her mounting terror, she forced herself to focus. Her body was sluggish from the chemical that had been used to knock her out, but her mind sharpened with a singular determination: escape.

She pushed herself up to her knees, using her bound hands against the floorboards. Scuttling around the barn, she made her way to a hole in a wall. Peering out, she could see a fence post far off in the distance. She must be on one of the ranches on the western side of the park. The sun rose over the eastern horizon, providing her bearings. But the location didn't matter if she couldn't run.

Marlee made her way around the room, bending to sweep the place for anything that could help her untie the binds. Under a workbench, she found an old, dusty glass soda bottle. She grasped it in one hand before swinging around to let it fly. Crouching to shield her face against the smashing glass, the bottle fragmented against the wall. Marlee hopped over and carefully picked up one of the sharpest pieces. Swallowing a burst of hope, she gripped it awkwardly, twisting her wrists to slice at the ropes. The jagged edges cut into her skin, but she kept going until the fibers frayed and snapped. Freed, she yanked the gag from her mouth and then attacked the ropes at her ankles.

She checked her wrists to make sure she wasn't bleeding from a vital artery and planned her next move before her captors returned.

But what about Nancy Sue? What about the dogs?

A vehicle rumbled in the distance, drawing closer. Marlee's heart slammed against her ribs. She had no time to figure out a plan. She had to act now.

Frantically, she scanned the barn for another way out. The door was too obvious and likely guarded, but the floorboards—some of them were loose. She darted to a section where the wood had rotted and pried at it with her fingers, lifting it just enough to reveal a crawl space beneath.

Just as she prepared to slide down, the sound of tires crunching on gravel froze her in place. A door creaked open, and Marlee decided not to alert to her disappearance just yet. Kicking the glass to the shadows but grabbing one sharp piece for a weapon, she raced back to the spot where she had awoken and stuffed the foul gag back in her mouth. With her hands and glass behind her, she pretended to still be knocked out.

The barn door opened, followed by the thud of something heavy being thrown inside.

A groan followed beside her.

Not something—someone.

Marlee remained motionless, pressing her eyes closed no matter how much she wanted to see who was there. Footsteps echoed until the person stepped outside, and then Charlie's voice cut through the silence.

"I better get double for delivering this guy, too."

Two doors slammed, and the vehicle engine roared to life and sped away.

Marlee's pulse thundered in her ears as she risked opening her eyes and hoping no one had remained behind. She slowly turned, inching forward to see what had been dumped beside her.

A choked gasp left her lips.

Hunter.

He lay unmoving, his body tied up completely with ropes.

Terror gripped her as she scrambled to his side, shaking him gently. "Hunter," she whispered urgently. "Hunter, wake up."

He groaned again. "Marlee? You're alive. You're here. I prayed so hard. Take the blind off so I can see you."

She did as he asked, and was greeted with his intense hazel eyes, but this time, she thought she saw something else in them.

Love?

No. She was just looking at her own reflection in his eyes.

"It's really you," he said with a sigh of relief.

She forced a shaky smile. "Yeah, it's me. We need to get out of here."

His gaze darted around the barn, his body tensing. He tried

to push himself up but faltered against the tight binds and wincing in pain.

Marlee grabbed her piece of glass. She worked the rope until it frayed and split, tearing the rest from him and quickly wrapping an arm around his shoulders to help him sit up.

"I…" he started, but his voice was hoarse, almost broken. He swallowed hard before whispering, "I love you."

Marlee stilled at the words she had longed to hear when she was younger, but pressed forward, knowing he was loopy. She let out a breathless chuckle. "They must have given you some potent drugs."

Hunter shook his head, though the movement seemed to take great effort. "No… I mean it." His eyes, now clearer, locked onto hers. "I should have told you before. Please forgive me for everything."

She pressed a hand to his chest, feeling his heartbeat beneath her palm. She had no time to process his confession, but something inside her softened, releasing the last fragments of caution she had for Hunter.

"I forgive you," she whispered. "For everything."

Marlee realized she meant it, too. For so long, she had blamed Hunter for Ben's death, but now she knew Ben needed to be the one to bear the responsibility. Ben and the drugs that had destroyed him. That Hunter had faced Ben's dealer and learned Ben owed a lot of money told Marlee that even Hunter hadn't known the breadth of the problem. Marlee had to believe if he had, he wouldn't have paid for that last lethal dose of drugs.

A weight seemed to lift from Hunter's shoulders. "Thank you, Marlee. I waited too long to make amends and wish…."

Marlee studied his beautiful eyes that held a longing in them she recognized…a longing for what might have been for them if they had faced their pain. But the sound of another vehicle approaching cut their reconciliation moment short.

Marlee's stomach clenched. "Get under the floorboards," she whispered urgently, guiding Hunter toward the loose board she'd uncovered earlier.

They barely had time to slip beneath the barn before they heard the vehicle's door open and slam shut. Marlee pressed herself low in the sand, hoping no snakes made this cool, dark space their habitat. She led the way toward the sunlight and peeked out, just in time to see Clint Jackson heft the rifle with his hand.

Marlee's fingers tightened into fists, her mind racing.

Clint lifted a gasoline can from the bed of his truck and stepped up, only a few feet from where they hid. He poured the liquid in slow, deliberate arcs along the barn's edges.

Marlee's blood ran cold.

He wasn't here to negotiate.

He was here to finish them.

Marlee whispered, "Jackson didn't want Nancy Sue."

"I pray that means she's safe," Hunter replied.

"Me too. I pray that, too." A peace Marlee hadn't felt in eight years flooded over her. She may have turned away from God, but He never left her side.

Hunter's warm smile only solidified that fact. He would know this more than anyone.

"Are you ready?" she asked.

Hunter squeezed her hand and nodded. "It's go-time."

Before Jackson could strike his match, Marlee got to her knees and lunged forward from their hiding place. With a desperate burst of energy, she tackled him from behind, knocking the rifle and gas can from his hands. They tumbled to the ground, grappling for control. Clint was stronger, but Marlee had something he didn't—pure determination to end this once and for all.

Hunter emerged from the crawl space, staggering but ready to jump into the fight. Together, they overpowered Clint, forcing him onto his stomach and securing his hands behind his back with the very ropes Marlee had cut Hunter from earlier.

Gasping for breath, she met Hunter's eyes.

"Meet Clint Jackson," she sneered, rubbing the drug lord's face in the dirt.

Hunter nodded, a small smile spreading on his lips. "Aren't you going to do the thing?"

"The thing?" Marlee squinted in confusion.

"Yeah, you know, the thing." His expression brightened until she caught on and laughed.

"Oh, yeah!" She lifted Clint's head by his long hair and said, "DEA, and you're under arrest."

"Love that." Hunter slapped his thigh, and Marlee grinned right back at him.

Dragging Clint to his feet, they hauled him toward his own truck and threw him into the back. Marlee slid into the driver's seat, heart pounding as she jammed the keys into the ignition.

They had one destination in mind.

The sheriff's office.

Nancy Sue was missing again. Without a second thought, Marlee sent up a prayer and let the old familiarity of a life walked with God calm her nerves as she drove out to civilization once again.

Hunter and Marlee rushed to the front doors of the sheriff's department, Clint Jackson staggering between them. His wrists were secured in ropes, and his face bore the bruises from their earlier struggle. Hunter didn't care if the man was hurting—he deserved worse. He found it interesting that Jackson was doing his own dirty work. Where were his men? Perhaps they knew this was a losing battle—kidnapping and killing a federal agent came at a higher price than Jackson could pay. Perhaps they'd packed it up for home.

Sheriff Hawkins was just locking up his office when they burst into the building. His gaze flickered over them, settling on Clint with mild surprise. "What's this?"

Hunter exhaled sharply, steadying himself before launching into an explanation. "We've been missing for the last few days. Kidnapped. Then last night, Marlee and I were locked up in a barn, and this piece of trash—" he yanked Clint forward "—was one of the men holding us. Clint Jackson is the drug dealer who put a hit out on Marlee."

"And he has our dogs somewhere," Marlee said. "We need him to talk."

Clint sneered, but the man knew enough to keep his mouth shut. He sent a lethal glare Marlee's way, but she didn't give him the time of day. Her strength continued to impress Hunter.

The sheriff's expression remained impassive as he waved over a deputy. "Take Jackson to holding." To Hunter he said, "Well, that explains why you haven't returned my calls. Agent Williams called me this morning, saying he couldn't track Marlee, either. I was about to start a search and rescue for the two of you."

Once Clint was escorted away, Hunter asked Hawkins, "No one from the SAR team put out an alert?"

Hawkins shook his head. "I had no idea you were missing."

Marlee stiffened beside Hunter. "A ranger was involved. She double-crossed us for Jackson's bounty. She has someone else she's working with. That person drugged me."

The sheriff huffed. "The park rangers reported that you two went off on your own to continue the search. I had no reason to believe anything was wrong at first. Sounds like the rangers had dollar signs in their eyes."

Realization dawned on Hunter like a gut punch. Was that why his SAR team hadn't sounded the alarm? Were they all in on it? He thought back to the last conversation he'd had with Michael—tense, full of accusations. Had Michael deliberately kept quiet? Had he been promised a cut?

Marlee must have been thinking the same thing, because she leaned closer, voice lowered. "Michael was the one who knew exactly where we were going. You don't think he had something to do with this, do you?"

Hunter's jaw tightened. He wanted to deny it, but doubt crept in. "I don't know," he admitted. "But I wouldn't put it past him right now. He's very upset that you're back in my life."

A pretty blush crept up Marlee's cheeks, but she quickly cleared her throat and put her focus back on Sheriff Hawkins.

Sheriff Hawkins asked, "Which rangers were involved?"

"Charlie Woodridge," Marlee replied.

Hawkins's face paled. "Charlie?"

Hunter nodded. "Yeah, surprising, isn't it?"

"But that's impossible." Sheriff Hawkins raced for the door. "She's about to be on live TV, taking credit for finding Nancy Sue. I was just heading over to the town hall for the news conference."

Marlee and Hunter exchanged a glance.

"The gall," she said, racing for the door. "I'll arrest that woman myself."

They all sprinted from the station and down the street where a small crowd had gathered in front of the town hall. Cameras flashed as reporters clamored for the best shot of Charlie, who stood confidently at the podium.

"I'm just grateful I could bring Nancy Sue Hartman home,"

Charlie announced, her voice dripping with false humility. "It was a tough search, but I never lost hope."

Hunter clenched his fists, his entire body coiling with fury. He moved to storm the stage, but Marlee grabbed his arm. "Not yet," she whispered. "Let her think we're dead."

He gritted his teeth but relented, stepping back into the shadows. He scanned the crowd, searching for familiar faces. Near the back, standing stiffly, were Michael and Elliott. Both men looked uneasy, shifting on their feet, their gazes darting toward the stage. Guilt? Did they know this was all a show?

Marlee whispered beside him, "Charlie's not a killer."

Hunter frowned. "She helped one. And she's definitely a kidnapper. She kidnapped us."

Marlee's upper lip curled in anger. "And now she's here, playing hero, reuniting Nancy Sue with her father. Despicable."

Hunter turned his attention back to the stage, searching for the little girl. He didn't see her.

Then Charlie gestured toward the town hall doors. "And now, I present Leon Carl and his little girl, Nancy Sue, reunited again."

The doors swung open, and Leon stepped out, carrying Nancy Sue in his arms. The little girl's face remained buried in his shoulder, but when she finally lifted her head, Hunter caught the shimmer of tears on her cheeks.

Leon spoke briefly, his voice tight. "Nancy Sue and I have been through a terrible ordeal. I ask for privacy as we heal."

Then, as quickly as they had appeared, he turned and disappeared back inside as reporters threw out questions that went unanswered.

Hunter's gut twisted. He studied the way Nancy Sue had clung to Leon, her small fingers gripping his shirt. It looked like trust. But something about it felt…off.

He whispered to Marlee, "She's scared."

She exhaled on a nod. "He's her legal father. There's not much we can do to change that. But we still have her DNA. One cheek swab from you, and we'll know for sure if you're her daddy. Do you want to know?"

Hunter stared at the closed doors of the town hall, conflicted. Marlee took his hand in hers and squeezed. Giving her his full attention, he said, "For Nancy Sue's safety, we have to know."

Marlee frowned. "Charlie had help. I hate to think Nancy Sue has just been handed over to her accomplice, but at this point, that scenario could very well be possible."

SEVENTEEN

Marlee paced the length of the stable at Hunter's ranch, her boots scuffing against the hay-strewn floor as she dialed the number for SAC Williams. The air smelled of fresh straw and horses, but the familiar scents did little to calm her racing mind. She held her breath as the line rang, exhaling only when the gruff voice of her superior answered.

"Price, you're alive. I don't like it when my agents go rogue."

"Kidnapped. Long story. Right now, I need Gustav's location. Jackson has him and Hunter's SAR bloodhound, Libby, holed up somewhere. Jackson's in custody but not talking. Can you check Gustav's tracker?"

"On it right now." SAC Williams typed while he spoke. "I looked into Leon Carl."

Marlee kept her voice low even though she was alone. "I also need everything you can dig up on Charlotte Woodridge. The woman kidnapped us, and I can't wait to cuff her and take her in. But I want to know who she is, besides the perky park ranger she poses as."

"You don't think she's the killer?"

"No, it looks like she kidnapped us for the money. And to claim she was the one who found Nancy Sue. I don't know how, but she's connected to the drug camp."

Williams was quiet for a moment before replying, "Well, Carl is clean. No criminal record, no outstanding debts, no red flags. Not even a parking ticket."

Marlee frowned, muttering, "That's impossible. There must be something on him."

"It does seem too perfect," Williams admitted. "Everything about him checks out, but that's the problem. It's almost like someone crafted an ideal background for him. No mistakes, no missteps, no gaps. It's contrived. Fabricated…on purpose."

A chill crept up Marlee's spine. "If that's the case, then we need to act fast. The child is with Carl now. If he's not who he says he is, and if Nancy Sue has been turned over to her mother's killer—"

"I know," Williams cut in. "I'll get on Woodridge's background right away. And here's Gustav's location. I'm texting it to you now. He looks to be at a ranch."

"Let me guess. On the western side of the park."

"You got it."

Marlee sighed in frustration. "Something tells me this entire case is being run out of one of those ranches. Can you get me a warrant? I'd like to look around."

"Absolutely. They've got our dog. I'll have it for you in a couple of hours. Be careful going in. Can you get backup from the sheriff?"

"I'm sure." Marlee hesitated before adding, "There's something else. I think Hunter is Nancy Sue's father. He's considering a paternity test."

There was a pause on the other end of the line. Then Williams said, "Interesting. Do you think he should be considered as a suspect?"

"No. From what I have seen, he should be only considered as her rightful parent." Marlee chewed her lip, staring out over the stalls. At one time, the thought would have devastated her.

When she and Hunter were younger, she'd wanted to be the only person in his world. The idea of him having a child with someone else would have crushed her.

But now, she needed to do everything she could to make it happen.

She let her head rest against a wooden beam and closed her eyes. "I know he'd be an amazing father. He protects the ones he loves. That's what he thought he was doing for Ben. He would lay down his life for those he loves…maybe even those he doesn't. But if Nancy Sue is his daughter, I know he'll cherish her forever."

For a moment, silence stretched on the line before Williams spoke again. "What about you? Don't you want to be cherished like that?"

Marlee's throat tightened at the unexpected question from her boss. Did she want that? That kind of unconditional love? Not just in general, but from Hunter?

Before she could answer, a change in the air made her turn. Hunter stood in the barn entrance, watching her. His piercing eyes, darkened by shadow and unreadable emotion, locked onto hers.

It was as if he'd heard every word.

Marlee took a steadying breath, her grip tightening on the phone. She didn't look away as she finally answered, "I once loved Hunter with my whole heart, but back then, it was only the idea of him. Now, I love him for who he really is. And I would be honored to be cherished by him."

Hunter took a slow step forward, his expression unreadable but intense. He crossed the space between them with careful deliberation, his gaze never wavering. When he reached her, he lifted his hands, cupping her cheeks, holding on as if she might run away. His thumbs brushed over her cheekbones, his breath warm against her skin.

"I love you, too," he whispered.

A chuckle sounded through the phone, reminding Marlee that SAC Williams was still on the line. "I'll check back in a little while. Be safe. Though I don't think Hunter's going to let you out of his sight anytime soon."

The call disconnected, but Marlee barely noticed. The moment the phone left her hand, dropping to the straw on the floor, Hunter closed the distance between them, his lips capturing hers in a kiss that stole away her breath and set her world right again.

Marlee hoped he would never let her go again, even if that was wishful thinking.

Hunter kissed Marlee as if he'd been starving for her all his life, which, deep down, he knew he had. The feel of her, the taste of her, everything about her consumed him. He poured every unspoken word, every buried emotion, into that kiss, afraid that if he let go, she would slip through his fingers.

When he finally pulled back, his forehead rested against hers as he caught his breath. "I've always loved you, Marlee. Always."

She let out a shaky exhale, her fingers still tangled in his shirt. "Hunter…"

"All those women, all the chasing?" he said, brushing his thumb along her jaw. "I think I see now. It was because I could never have you. I spent years looking for someone like you, when all along, it was impossible, because there's no one like you."

Her eyes shimmered with unshed tears, and he kissed her again, deep and unyielding. A quiet sob escaped her, and he felt her tears against his skin. It wasn't just her crying—his own tears were mixing with hers. He had dreamed of this moment, of finding love, imagined it a thousand different ways, but nothing prepared him for his true love being Marlee Price. It was not a door he would have tried to open. It was like…

It was like God had to be the one to open it for him.

And Hunter knew without a doubt that He just had.

Hunter pulled back just enough to look into Marlee's eyes. "I honored Ben's wishes to keep my distance from you," he admitted, his voice hoarse with emotion. "Do you think he would give us his blessing now?"

Marlee let out a trembling breath, her hands coming up to cradle his face. "I put Ben on a pedestal when I shouldn't have. Since his death, I haven't rested—chasing down every drug operation as if it would undo my mistake of not seeing his problem sooner. But maybe if I hadn't given him such an honor, he'd still be here. Maybe if we had been honest with him…he would have given us his blessing then. I think he'd want me to be happy. And I think he'd want you to be happy, too."

"Do I make you happy, Marlee?"

She flashed a beaming, bright smile at him that brought back so many memories. "You always did."

Emotion swelled in his chest, and he couldn't hold back any longer. He kissed her again, slower this time, as if savoring a dream finally turned real. Every memory of her laughter, of her chasing him on the football field as kids, flooded his mind. He had let her catch him when they were little, but never off the field as they got older. He could never allow her to come closer than Ben would allow. But Hunter was done running now.

He pulled back just enough to murmur against her lips, "All I ever wanted was to let you catch me."

Marlee let out a soft laugh, her fingers sliding into his hair, entwining her fingertips into his curls at his neck. His nerve endings felt like live wires. "Consider yourself caught," she said.

A deep chuckle rumbled in his chest, but just as he was about to pull her close again, his phone buzzed against his hip. He groaned close to her lips, reluctant to end their moment. His horse nickered from a nearby stall, as if sharing his frustration.

Reluctantly, he pulled away and reached for his phone, glancing at the screen. His jaw tightened. "It's Michael."

Marlee straightened, sensing the change in his demeanor. "Answer it."

Hunter swiped to accept the call. "Michael?"

"We need to talk. Now. Alone." Michael's voice was tight, urgent.

Hunter's muscles coiled with tension. "About what?"

"The truth. It's time you knew it all. Especially about that woman and her family you think you love so much. When all they did was leave you hurting and carrying the bag."

"Bag? What are you talking about? What bag?"

"Just meet me at the ranger station in thirty minutes."

The line went dead before Hunter could respond.

He lowered the phone, his mind already racing. Why was Michael demanding to meet alone? Why the demand for secrecy? And what bag was left for Hunter to carry?

Marlee crossed her arms, already stepping away from him. "That sounded ominous."

"Yeah," Hunter muttered, shoving the phone back into his pocket and reaching for her hand, needing to touch her. "And I don't like it."

She studied him, worry flickering in her gaze. "Do you think he had something to do with our kidnapping? With Clint Jackson showing up at that barn?"

Hunter clenched his jaw at the idea that had crossed his

mind since the press conference. “I don’t know. But if he did, I’ll find out. He might just be upset that I haven’t reached out to tell him what happened to us. He still believes we went off on our own. We got into a brief fight before I left.”

She nodded, clearly remembering what had been said in the sheriff’s office earlier. “I’m going with you.”

“Marlee—”

“No,” she cut in, stepping closer. “We’re in this together. Unless you didn’t mean what you just said.”

“Of course I did. I meant every word.” He exhaled heavily. He wanted to keep her safe, but he also knew better than to argue with her when she had that determined set to her jaw. Besides, she had been right about staying together back at the camp. They should have made their escape together. They would have been able to overtake Charlie and her accomplice if they had.

“Fine,” he conceded. “But we’re going in prepared.”

She gave a sharp nod, already reaching for her gun, a piece she’d selected from his gun cabinet the moment they had arrived. “Always. And after, we go get our dogs.” She picked up her phone from the straw and brought her screen to life. A picture of Gustav was pinned to a map, right outside the park.

Hunter studied the map. “Interesting. They weren’t too far from us when we were in that barn. I’d like to meet the owner of that ranch. The guards wore the brand on their bandannas.”

“You can ask all your questions in a little while. I have a warrant coming.”

Hunter smiled at this powerhouse of a woman. “Of course you do. Have I told you how proud I am of you? Though not surprised, you grew into this brave, heroic law-woman. It boggles my mind that you would want someone like me.”

She paused as she pocketed her phone, a tilt to her head. “You mean someone who reminds me about empathy? That life isn't black and white, and it's okay to rest? That I'm not a machine, I'm alive? That I've been hurting since the night you turned me away?" Marlee touched his chest, and he knew she could feel the way his heart raced in her presence. Hunter covered her hand, wanting to be honest about everything now.

He took her hand and led her from the barn to his truck, pausing at the passenger door.

"Marlee, I'm sorry about that night. I nearly went after you after I closed the door. You should know, I sent that girl home and vowed to stop chasing women from then on. I started dating Donna exclusively after. I know you don't want to talk about God—"

"No. I do," Marlee said, squeezing his hand. "I've pushed Him away for as long as I have been pushing you away. Neither were a good idea. I loved the man you once were, but I am in love with the man God has made you into."

"Even though I slipped up that night with Donna?"

"Are you sorry about that night?"

Hunter pressed his lips. "Yes, wholeheartedly. But if Nancy Sue is my daughter, I won't be sorry about her. She's not a mistake."

Marlee smiled, lighting her eyes. She shook her head and laughed. "Another reason I love you is your ability to see the truth. Babies are never a mistake."

"They're a blessing."

"Are you going to get tested?"

Hunter nodded emphatically, having no inhibitions for holding back any longer. "I love her, Marlee," he whispered. "Even if she's not mine, I already love her."

"She is a special girl. She takes after her father. Her heart is just like yours."

Marlee frowned. "Nancy Sue told me they were running

from someone. And we're going to find out who that was. I won't stop until I do."

Hunter pulled Marlee close, dropping his face into the crook of her neck and breathing deeply from the strength she exuded. Hunter didn't doubt Marlee's ability to always get her bad guy and believed this case would be no different.

But she wouldn't do it just out of duty. She would do it because she loved him.

Hunter stepped back and opened her door for her to climb in. He checked his own weapon at his side. He had a bad feeling about this meeting with Michael. Something was off. Whatever Michael wanted to say, Hunter had a sinking suspicion it was about to change everything.

But he would not let it come between him and Marlee.

Nothing and no one would separate them ever again. That was one promise Hunter never intended to break.

EIGHTEEN

Marlee strode into the ranger station beside Hunter, bracing for an unpleasant encounter with Michael but also ready to make amends with this man who was Hunter's friend. In the dimly lit room, Michael sat waiting at the conference table, arms crossed over his chest, his face set in a deep scowl. The air crackled with tension, and she figured he wasn't looking for amends at the moment.

She also wasn't about to give the man an easy out, especially if he had anything to do with their kidnapping. Marlee pulled out a chair and sat down, meeting Michael's glare with an unflinching stare of her own. Hunter remained standing beside her, a picture of strength together.

"You're angry Hunter brought me," she said. "Why don't you like me, Michael?"

Michael leaned forward and shot back, "I was there for him when you weren't. I was the one who picked up the pieces. When Ben's drug dealer came knocking for his debts, I was the one who handled the mess your brother made."

Marlee's breath caught. She glanced at Hunter, who had yet to take a seat.

Now he did.

"You paid Ben's debts?" Marlee asked, stunned. She had planned to call her parents, to ask if anyone had ever come looking for the money he owed. But now she saw the answer standing right in front of her. It was Michael who had paid the drug dealer?

She swallowed hard. "You protected Hunter," she murmured, realization settling in.

Michael's expression darkened. "Someone had to."

Hunter spoke, his voice low and tight. "You knew about Ben's debts?"

Michael rolled his eyes with an exasperated exhale. "Of course I did. That dealer came knocking for you one day. But I took care of it. Made a deal…to protect you."

"Why didn't you tell me?" Hunter asked, his tone laced with disbelief.

Michael looked away. "It wasn't that simple."

"Then break it down for me."

Michael hesitated, but Marlee leaned forward, her voice steady and sure. "Hunter deserves to know the truth, Michael. All of it."

Michael's lips pressed into a thin line before he finally muttered, "The dealer wanted you out of Donna's life. All I had to do was tell her the truth about you and the debt was gone."

The words hung in the air, heavy and full of accusations.

Marlee's brows knit together. "What truth?"

Hunter's face paled as understanding dawned on his face. "You told her about my past relationships."

Michael sputtered. "*Relationships* is saying it nicely. I told her about the parties and how you would never be faithful to her. That she was just another of your conquests."

Hunter's fists clenched. "That's why she left me."

Marlee watched the realization cut through him like a blade. She had seen Hunter take on impossible rescues and walk straight into danger without hesitation. But this broke him. He gave empathy so freely, but his friend didn't afford him the same. She couldn't sit back and allow Michael to steal this from Hunter.

"How could you?" she asked. "What kind of friend are you?"

Michael exhaled sharply. "You don't get it. That dealer would not let it go. He would have come for Hunter next. Or Ben's family. You. Your parents. He was going to kill Hunter. He offered me a deal, and I took it. I did what I had to do to keep him alive."

Hunter shook his head, his voice barely above a whisper. "By ruining my life?"

"You ruined your life when you didn't sign up for the draft. Your own father would agree. And now you're doing it again for her."

Marlee's phone buzzed in her pocket, the sound jarring against the thick accusation. She checked it and read a message from SAC Williams.

"The warrant is ready," she announced. "The sheriff's department is on their way to the ranch."

Hunter straightened, his face hardened into determination. "It's time to get our dogs. Our real loyal companions."

Michael pushed away from the table. "I'm coming with you."

Hunter didn't hesitate. "No, you're not. You're fired."

Michael's eyes burned with frustration. "Hunter—"

"Your kind of help is sabotage," Hunter cut him off. "I don't need it anymore."

Michael threw his hands up. "You're making a mistake. I protected you from being killed."

"No," Hunter said, his voice cold. "I would have gladly paid Ben's debts myself rather than have you tarnish my name with Donna."

"I only told her the truth about you. It wasn't like I was

lying. You were a player. We both knew you always would be." Michael's eyebrows raised as though he expected Hunter to deny his sins.

Hunter stood, gripping the back of his chair. "Except you forgot one very important detail. Jesus had paid my debts. I was trying to turn my life around. Did I mess up? Yes, and I have had to accept the consequences for that. But my past didn't define me anymore. I was given another chance to get it right. That's what His sacrifice does for us, and you took that gift away from me."

Marlee rose from her chair, her mind spinning. She was so proud of Hunter at that moment, but she also wondered why would Ben's dealer want Donna to know about Hunter's past? How would keeping them apart benefit the man? And who was he?

She didn't have the answers. Not yet. And right now, she could only focus on one thing.

Getting her K-9 back.

She led the way to the door. Just as she turned the knob, someone on the other side pulled the door from her grasp.

It took less than two seconds to register that Charlie Woodridge was holding the door. It took Charlie two more seconds to realize that Marlee and Hunter were still alive. All color drained from her face, and her bulging eyes looked like a few blood vessels could break.

Charlie let the door go and bolted back to her SUV, running with nowhere to hide.

"Run all you want, Woodridge. I'm coming for you!" Marlee shouted. "Get your affairs in order. You're going away for a long time."

"You don't want to arrest her?" Hunter asked as they watched her drive away, swerving haphazardly. She was running scared.

Marlee smirked at him. "Did you see the look on her face? Gustav is going to love chasing her down. It'll be a treat for him."

"Well, he sure deserves one after everything he's been through."

"Yup. Let's go get our dogs. Then it's hunting time."

Hunter stepped out of the vehicle at the same time Sheriff Hawkins and his two deputies, Willis and Montgomery, pulled up. The crunch of gravel beneath their boots echoed in the dry desert air, but Hunter barely noticed. The ranch house at the Lone Vida loomed ahead, its size and grandeur a stark contrast to the growing storm in his gut. He was surrounded by men he'd once called friends, yet right now, he wasn't sure who he could trust. Michael's betrayal cut deep, stealing the breath from his lungs.

Marlee, standing beside him, exuded the quiet confidence he needed right now. He let her take the lead, his own mind too clouded by anger and suspicion to think clearly.

She stepped up to the door, knocking sharply. "DEA! We have a warrant to search the premises."

Moments later, it creaked open, revealing a small, frazzled woman. Her eyes widened at the sight of the sheriff's badge and the warrant in Marlee's hand.

"S-señora?" the woman stammered. "Please, come inside. My boss, a dog has bitten him—" she continued in broken English.

Marlee smirked. "That's what my dog is trained to do. Especially when he's being held hostage. Where is he?"

Marlee whistled, and immediately Gustav could be heard barking from somewhere in the back of the house.

But he didn't come to them.

Marlee picked up her steps to find him, and Hunter kept

up with her, passing through the expansive foyer toward the harsh voice of a man shouting in pain. Racing over marble flooring and under crystal chandeliers that alluded to a lot of drug money passing through these doors, they entered the solarium at the back of the house.

But it was not the German shepherd pinning the man down.

It was Libby.

Hunter's sweet, mild-mannered bloodhound growled over the man in the middle of the room as the man cried out, "Get her off me!"

"Off!" Hunter shouted, but didn't want to scold his dog. This kidnapper deserved every bite.

As the man sat on the floor, clutching his bleeding arm, pain and fury evident in his expression, Hunter's stomach twisted. Libby wasn't a protector K-9. She was a tracker. She'd only bite if someone stood in the way of her doing her job.

Which meant she had found something.

Marlee stepped forward, folding her arms. "Looks like your dog got to him before we did. Good dog, Libby."

The man scowled. "Get that mutt away from me!"

"Where's the German shepherd?" Marlee asked.

"In the garage. Get them both out of here! I'm not some dog babysitter. The guy who was supposed to come get them never showed."

"He's in jail for attempted murder. A friend of yours?" Marlee deadpanned.

"Never met him." The guy shook his head. "I let the dogs stay here for a favor for an old army buddy. I didn't know they were attack dogs."

"They're not. They're police working dogs. Are you the homeowner?" Marlee held up the warrant. "Mr. Louis Malcolm?"

"Yes. What is that?"

"A warrant to search the premises, both inside and out, including all vehicles and outbuildings. Will we find anything illegal when we do our search?"

As the homeowner complained and stated he'd done nothing wrong, Hunter gave his attention to his dog. She was agitated, but whatever caused it went beyond irritation with Mr. Malcolm. Hunter knelt beside Libby, running a hand over her head. She turned with her typical alerting excitement. "What is it, girl? What did you find?"

Libby turned away from the man and trotted toward the hallway. Hunter exchanged a glance with Marlee before following. Sheriff Hawkins and the deputies stayed behind to restrain the man, who grew angrier and more defiant over having his home searched, but Hunter let the officers handle him. Hunter was search and rescue and would focus on what his dog had found.

Libby led them through the house, nose to the floor, tail rigid. She halted outside a closed door, letting out a single, sharp bark.

Hunter reached for the doorknob, but it was locked. He didn't hesitate—he rammed his shoulder into the wood, sending the door splintering open.

Inside, the room was a tidy child's bedroom with pink decor and a canopy bed—all in full princess fashion. Libby raced inside and sat by the closet door, giving her proud bark of accomplishment.

Hunter's blood turned to ice. He stalked forward, circling the room, wondering if Nancy Sue had been there.

He stepped in without a word and went right to the closet, opening it wide.

"Good find, Libby." He held up the pink backpack, reaching in to remove a single rainbow sneaker.

"I assume that's the bag and shoe found at the murder scene," Marlee said.

"It was taken after I was clocked in the head with a rock," Hunter said. "Looks like Mr. Malcolm has more to tell us."

Hunter stormed back toward the man in the solarium. Sheriff Hawkins restrained him, but he still squirmed, his eyes darting around in panic.

Hunter demanded, "How do you know Nancy Sue Hartman?"

The man hesitated, but then his jaw tightened with a lift to his chin. "I don't know who you're talking about."

Hunter tossed the backpack onto the floor between them. "Then explain this. This bag and shoe were taken from a murder scene. They're now in your house. Did you kill Donna Hartman and kidnap her daughter?"

The man's gaze flickered to the bag, and in that instant, Hunter knew he was going to lie. He grabbed the front of his shirt, hauling him up. "Tell me the truth!"

"Okay!" the man gasped, and his face paled. "I didn't touch the kid! And I didn't kill anyone. I was just following orders to get her things from the canyon."

Hunter shoved him back against the couch. "Whose orders?"

The man swallowed hard. "I—I can't say."

"I want a name. Now!"

Louis Malcolm huffed, with a smirk growing on his lips. Hunter barely controlled himself from wiping it off. "He goes by Lone Ranger. And that's all I'm telling you. You'll need more than a warrant to get me to turn on a friend."

Hunter held him steady. "Your friend's in a lot of trouble. Murder and kidnapping are just the beginning. A genuine friend would make sure his buddy faced the light. Covering for him will only hurt both of you. Trust me on that. The truth will come out. So do your friend a favor and tell us what he's into."

Marlee placed her hand over her sidearm, standing tall with a threatening presence of authority. "Is it drugs? Smuggling?"

"He's into everything," the man said quickly, his voice losing its edge. "Drugs, smuggling, weapons—you name it. He has connections. He asked me to kill the trail. That's it."

Hunter's mind reeled. None of this made sense. Lone Ranger? Was this the man at the center of everything? The one pulling the strings?

"And Donna?" Hunter's voice was tight, controlled. "Did he order her killed?"

The man hesitated. "I was ordered to kill the trail so no one could follow it to the camp. That's it."

Hunter's breath came in short, shallow bursts. "And the other women? The reporter? The undercover cop?"

The man lowered his gaze. "The narc got herself killed. She tried to escape with the kid when she was brought to the trailer. That was her own fault. I don't know why the reporter was killed. My guess is she was snooping around where she didn't belong."

"Was Nancy Sue here?"

Hunter felt Marlee shift beside him, but he couldn't look at her. His mind was whirling, rage simmering beneath his skin. He needed to know what happened to her after she was taken that night. What horrid experiences befell her?

"I never met her. I was told to get the backpack. That's all."

"Right, for your friend with no name. I need a name. His real name. If you won't do it for your friend, do it for a little girl who's innocent in all this. Did you know he sold her to a drug encampment for manual labor?" Hunter pressed, his patience razor-thin.

Louis's head jerked high, a stunned expression on his face. Now Hunter was getting somewhere.

The man opened his mouth, but before he could speak, the room exploded with noise.

Gunfire shattered the window, a hail of bullets tearing through the space as everyone lunged to the floor while glass rained around them.

The man let out a choked cry, his body jerking violently before he collapsed in a heap. Blood pooled around him, his secrets dying with him.

Hunter rolled onto his side, his heart pounding, to see Marlee on her back. “Marlee! Are you hit?”

She didn’t answer, but Gustav started barking again from the garage.

Dread coiled in his stomach as her face became tight with pain, her lips pressed into a thin line. And then he saw it—the red blooming across the front of her shirt.

His breath caught. “No, no, no!”

Marlee blinked at him, looking stunned. Panic surged through him as he pressed his hands against her shoulder, trying to stop the bleeding.

“Stay with me, Marlee. Don’t you dare—”

Her hand weakly gripped his wrist, her fingers trembling. “Call SAC Williams,” she whispered and winced. “Get me my dog.” She tried to smile but failed in her pain. “I want… him with me.”

Hunter clenched his jaw, swallowing back the terror clawing at his throat. He needed to get her out of here. Now.

Sheriff Hawkins was already shouting orders to his deputies, but Hunter barely heard them. All that mattered was Marlee.

Suddenly, Gustav came running and sniffed Marlee before laying his head on her stomach. Instantly, she relaxed and closed her eyes.

But would they close forever?

Hunter bowed his head and prayed for Him to not close this door so soon.

NINETEEN

Marlee gritted her teeth against the burning pain searing through her shoulder. She refused to let it take her down, to ruin the future she hoped to have with Hunter. She had to fight.

The bullet was lodged deep, and every breath sent a fresh wave of agony through her body, but she wouldn't let it stop her. Yet she also had to be reasonable. She was losing a lot of blood and could feel her body weakening by the second. In the distance, she could hear the sheriff making the call she'd asked for.

"SAC Williams, Sheriff Hawkins here. Agent Price took a hit. She's conscious but wants me to relay the details. I'm putting you on speaker." Sheriff Hawkins held the phone out for all to speak and hear. "Do you hear us?"

The response came through almost immediately. "Loud and clear. What's the status?"

Sheriff Hawkins continued, "Before the homeowner was killed, he gave us a name—Lone Ranger. Whoever this guy is, he's the one running everything. Drugs, smuggling, weapons. Have you heard the name before?"

A beat of silence passed before SAC Williams responded. "Yes. I remember an old case of an Army Ranger who went by that name. Could be connected."

"Ex-military?" Hunter said, his voice so close to her, it

made her jolt, but then instant peace came over her. Hunter was beside her. She could fight this, knowing he was with her. He continued, "I thought so in the first shootout with a sniper in a possible ghillie suit. He had good aim."

Marlee frowned, remembering how Hunter had kept his pain to himself out of concern for her, even when she treated him with disdain. She forced her eyes open and locked her gaze on him. If she bled out, she wanted his face to be the last one she saw.

The intensity staring back at her encouraged her to fight. She still had work to do.

SAC Williams spoke. "The Lone Ranger was a dishonorably discharged drug dealer. I remember laughing at the name. He went after new recruits and college kids. Real creep."

Hunter jutted his chin at Malcolm's dead body. "Louis here said he did a favor to an old army buddy. Sounds like the same guy to me."

Marlee tried to nod and whispered, "SAC Williams, we need a name. Also…what about Charlotte Woodridge?"

Hunter asked louder for her.

SAC Williams replied, "She's clean. But Donna… Turns out she had a brother. A guy named Leonard Carl Hartman."

Marlee's blood ran cold. "Say that…name again?" She spoke louder through the pain.

"You heard me right. Leonard Carl Hartman. He did time years ago for child smuggling. I'm texting you a picture now for confirmation."

The phone pinged instantly and up popped an old booking photo of Leon Carl.

"It's him," she whispered.

Hunter said, "Leon Carl is Donna's brother. Not her boyfriend, though she let everyone think he was. She let Nancy Sue think he was her father. Why?"

Hunter's face darkened, his grip on her tightening. He had to be stunned by this information.

"Donna," he murmured. "She was protecting her brother by giving him an alias. She ruined my child-smuggling case, remember? It's what broke us up the first time. I was ready to take down the operation, and by the time we got there, they had vanished. She tipped them off."

Marlee swallowed hard and used all her strength to speak. "She tipped her brother off? So it wasn't about getting the story at all… Maybe she didn't want Leon to go back to jail. SAC Williams, was Leonard Carl Hartman ever in the Army? Is he the Lone Ranger?"

"I'm a step ahead of you. And yes, he was. I'm sure he's the illustrious Lone Ranger."

The pieces were falling into place, but the picture they painted was worse than Marlee could imagine. If what she was thinking, Donna didn't end her relationship with Hunter because of what Michael had told her. She'd ended it to keep him from ever finding out who her brother was. Which also meant Hunter could never know about his child.

Sirens blared in the distance, growing louder by the second. The ambulance was close. Hunter shifted beside her, his hand never leaving her wound.

"You're gonna be okay," he promised.

Marlee forced a smile, feeling her eyes close. "I love you," she whispered. "If anything happens…"

"No, you're going to be fine."

"Listen to me. You've got to get Nancy Sue…away from… that man."

The paramedics entered the house, their expressions urgent as they assessed her wound. Hunter refused to move from her side as they transferred her onto a stretcher. Gustav never leaving her side, either, all the way to the ambulance.

As the ambulance doors shut, Marlee turned her head, her gaze locking onto Hunter's. Her vision swam, but she fought to stay conscious. "There's only one way to get Nancy Sue away from Leon Carl," she murmured, her words slurring slightly.

Hunter leaned closer. "I know."

Marlee blinked up at him, her strength fading. "Prove you're her father. And take down the man you were meant to stop six years ago."

"I will."

As darkness finally pulled her under, Hunter's determined face was the last thing she saw.

Hunter sat in the stiff plastic chair, his elbows resting on his knees, hands clasped together in silent prayer. The hospital waiting room was quiet except for the occasional beep of machines down the hall and the distant murmur of voices. He had just come from the lab, where a nurse had drawn his blood for the paternity test. Thirty minutes. That was all the time standing between him and his ability to claim Nancy Sue as his.

That and proving the man who had custody of her was a criminal.

Hunter's leg bounced anxiously as he rubbed a hand down his face.

Please, God, keep her safe until I can get to her.

It wasn't just the blood test that made his stomach churn—it was Marlee. She was in surgery, and until the doctors came out with an update, he felt like he was drowning in helplessness. The image of her blood staining her shirt, draining out of her body, was burned into his memory. He could still feel the strength of her body going slack against him. And yet, she still continued to do her job right until she'd passed out in the ambulance.

The double doors to the surgery ward swung open, and a nurse stepped out. "Hunter Shelton?"

He shot to his feet. "That's me."

"Marlee's out of surgery and waking up in recovery. You can see her now."

Relief rushed through him so fast his knees nearly buckled. He strode down the hallway, his pulse hammering as he was led into a dimly lit room. Marlee lay on the hospital bed, her blond hair tousled against the pillow, her skin pale while her chest rose and fell in steady breaths.

He pulled up a chair beside her bed and took her hand gently in his. He had almost lost her. The thought nearly undid him. He closed his eyes, pressing his forehead to the back of her hand, whispering a prayer of gratitude.

His phone vibrated against his thigh, and he pulled it out to read the caller I.D.

Sheriff Hawkins.

"Yeah?" Hunter answered, voice tight with emotion.

"Congratulations, Hunter," the sheriff said, his voice gruff but carrying a note of warmth. "You're a father. The test came back positive. Nancy Sue is yours, as if any of us thought otherwise."

The words hit him like a freight train. His breath caught in his throat. He squeezed his eyes shut as a wave of emotion surged through him—relief, joy, fear and an overwhelming sense of responsibility.

"Hunter? You there?" Hawkins asked.

Hunter cleared his throat, forcing himself to speak past the lump forming. "Yeah, I'm here."

"I'm heading to Leon's place now to get the child. I'll update you soon. As Donna's brother, he has no legal parental rights. If wants them, he'll have to fight you for them in court."

"Let him try. Thank you, Hawkins. Get her home safe. Don't scare her. She's been through so much."

The call disconnected, and Hunter sat frozen, the phone

still in his grip. He was a father. Nancy Sue was his little girl. His daughter.

Tears burned his eyes as he turned back to Marlee, her fingers twitching slightly in his hold. He had spent so many years running from things—his past, his mistakes, his feelings for Marlee. But this? This was something he wanted to run toward.

Marlee's eyelids fluttered, and she let out a quiet groan. Slowly, her lashes lifted, and her drowsy gaze settled on him. "Hunter?"

A weak smile tugged at his lips. "I'm here, sweetheart."

She blinked slowly, as if trying to clear the haze of anesthesia. Then her eyes narrowed slightly as she took in the moisture on his cheeks. "Am I dead?"

A startled laugh escaped him. "No," he said, brushing his knuckles against her cheek. "I just found out Nancy Sue is my little girl."

A slow, sleepy smile spread across her face. "I knew it."

Hunter swallowed the knot in his throat, overwhelmed by everything he felt at that moment. He kissed the back of her hand, his throat thick with emotion. "I can only think of one other thing that would make me happier."

Marlee's smile widened just a fraction, her fingers curling weakly around his. "What's that?"

Hunter leaned in, pressing his forehead gently against hers. "You. In my life forever. But I come with a child now."

Marlee smiled wider. "The most precious little girl I've ever met. Are you asking me what I think you're asking? Are you asking me to…marry you?"

"Marry me and help me raise Nancy Sue. Together. She adores you. I watched the two of you, and how she slept so peacefully in your arms. In a situation that terrified her, you comforted her with security. But I know, I'm asking a lot, so I understand if you need to think—"

"Yes. Yes. I don't have to think about anything." Tears fell from her eyes and trickled into her hair at her temples. "I love you, Hunter. And I love your little girl. I promise that will never change."

Hunter leaned in to capture her lips just as his phone vibrated again. Growling, he said, "Don't move."

"Like I could if I wanted to." Marlee rolled her eyes.

Hunter smirked, feeling light and excited as he accepted the call from Sheriff Hawkins. "Do you have her?"

"She's gone."

"What?"

"The place was empty. Swept clean. Not even a crumb left behind. They're gone. Both of them. I'm sorry, Hunter. Leon Carl tricked us all."

Hunter ended the call, sitting in a daze. "My little girl's been kidnapped…again."

Marlee moved to sit up, but winced as she did.

"Get Libby and your team over there," she demanded. "Bring me my clothes. We have a trail to pick up before it runs cold."

TWENTY

Marlee stepped out of the hospital doors, ignoring the tight pull of stitches in her shoulder and the dull throb radiating down her arm. The doctors had warned her not to leave, but they didn't understand—there was no time to rest. Nancy Sue was still out there, and every second wasted was a second too long.

Gustav stayed close, his large frame brushing against her leg as they moved across the sidewalk to Hunter's loaned police car. She'd kept Gustav off leash, knowing she might need her right hand free for her gun if things went south. Her left arm was useless, strapped against her torso to keep her from doing any further damage, but her right was at the ready. And if she couldn't rely on her own strength, she knew she could rely on Gustav.

Her phone buzzed in her pocket, and she yanked it free, seeing SAC Williams's name flash across the screen. She braced herself as she answered.

"Price." His voice came sharp and unimpressed. She knew he might have a thing or two to say about her having left the hospital, but to her surprise, he just sighed and said, "Beth Kline. She and Donna were college roommates, worked together at the station until Donna's death."

Marlee's brow furrowed. "Yeah, I know."

"But get this—Beth Kline was listed as the emergency contact on Nancy Sue's school account."

Marlee came to an abrupt stop. Gustav pressed against her leg, sensing her tension.

"She wasn't killed because she let my location slip on the news," she realized aloud. "She was killed because she was looking for Nancy Sue, too."

Williams made a sound of agreement. "She was a friend. A good one, even if she outed your location. She went looking for the child on her own, and it got her killed."

"If Beth knew what Leon Carl was up to, she would have kept notes or collected evidence. And if she kept notes and evidence, they're at her home."

"I already called the sheriff. They're en route," Williams said. "But Marlee, I want you back in that hospital bed right now. And that's an order."

"Text me the address." She hung up before he could argue further, shoving the phone into her pocket and heading for Hunter's car.

Hunter opened the passenger door for her. His jaw clenched as he took her in, sighing at her bandaged arm. "I don't like this," he said as she slid into the passenger seat, letting Gustav climb in the back seat with Libby.

"You don't have to," she replied as her phone buzzed. She turned it to face him for him to see their first stop. "You just have to drive."

"Where's that to?"

"Beth Kline's house. I got a lead."

Once behind the wheel, Hunter stopped arguing with her. With a curt nod, he shifted into gear and pulled onto the road.

The drive to Beth Kline's house was tense. Hunter cast frequent glances at her, his worry palpable, but he said nothing. Marlee smiled to herself, feeling so loved and protected by him. She'd been so tough and strong for so many years, she never knew what it would feel like to have someone to support her.

They pulled up to the modest suburban home. "Let's hope she left us a trail."

Hunter killed the engine. It was obvious they weren't the first people here. The front door was ajar, the frame splintered, and inside, drawers had been yanked open, papers scattered across the floor.

"We're too far behind Leon," Marlee muttered, stepping through the house with her K-9 by her side.

Hunter was close by so he could support her in an instant, hand hovering near his holster. "He was looking for something."

"To make sure no one else found it."

The moment Libby entered the house, her posture changed. Marlee recognized the body language instantly—she had a scent. "She's tracking."

Hunter nodded. "What is it, girl?"

Libby let out a low, eager whine and hurried through the house, sniffing her way to the back. Hunter and Marlee followed.

They reached the kitchen, and Libby stopped in front of the back door. The dog scratched at it, whining more urgently.

Hunter reached forward, yanking the door open, and out on the stoop was a half-eaten lollipop, discarded.

Marlee's breath caught. She picked up the candy by the stick and touched the top. "Still wet and sticky. She was here. And recently."

Hunter dropped the candy into a plastic bag. "I'd say the trail just got warm again."

"Let's have her keep searching."

They returned inside and let Libby continue her sniffing.

"What did Leon want in here? And did he find it?" Marlee crossed the kitchen, noticing the drawers and cabinets all open, some dumped on the floor. She stepped through the house, noticing how every room had been tossed, each one aggressively, as though the searcher wasn't finding what he was after.

"He didn't find it," she surmised. "Whatever it was, he left empty-handed."

Hunter stepped up beside her and scanned from the ceiling to the floor. "If Beth Kline was anything like Donna, she would know how to hide her evidence. There could be no chance of the story being leaked before she was ready to share all she had."

"And where might that place be?"

"I'll be right back." Hunter walked out the front door to his car. He pulled out his backpack and removed the picture he had taken from Donna's house, the one with her and Nancy Sue. Returning, he knelt next to Libby, giving her time with a fresh scent.

Donna's.

Immediately, Libby lifted her nose in the air, then dropped it to the floor, huffing and snorting in all directions.

Libby scuffled down the hall, sniffing the wood floors from left to right. Suddenly, she lifted her snout up the wall. In the next second, she began jumping on all fours and barking while also sticking her nose in the air.

"It's above," Hunter said, racing forward to calm his dog and remove her from the hunt.

Marlee studied the ceiling, seeing no type of opening or vent. "It's behind the wall?"

Hunter pointed straight up. "Attic. If Libby had longer legs, she would have jumped even higher."

"What she lacks in height, she makes up for in smarts."

Marlee entered the next room, looking for attic access. She found it in the closet.

Hunter grabbed an overturned chair. "Keep watch."

Then he was up and in the ceiling, lightning quick. He thudded around for a few minutes, hit his head once and grunted, before he called out that he had found something.

"What is it?" Marlee asked.

"Too dark up here. I'll send it down."

His legs dangled out of the opening as he passed down a brown paper bag. Marlee took it from him, thinking it weighed less than five pounds. She waited until he descended before opening it.

"Typically, I'm finding drug-stash places. So, here, you do the honors." Marlee passed the bag back to him. "This is your case."

Hunter took a deep breath before uncurling the rolled paper. He looked inside and squinted. "That's weird."

Marlee tried to peek. "Weird wasn't the reaction I was expecting. What is it?"

"We gave Sheriff Hawkins Donna's journal after you found it in her room, right?" Hunter reached inside the bag.

"Yes, immediately. In case there was something in it that would help with the case. Why?"

Hunter removed the same book with the bluebonnets they had found at Donna's house. "Well, if the sheriff has Donna's diary, then apparently, the women had matching journals."

Marlee took the book and opened it with her one hand, the pages splayed wide, and immediately she saw the difference. The words *my brother Leonard* jumped out at her.

"No, *this* is Donna's journal. The other was a fake, maybe planted to throw us off the trail. Listen to this… Donna says she wished she never stopped you from arresting Leonard." Marlee let more pages flip. "It's all here, Hunter. She says

Leonard threatened to take Nancy Sue and sell her." Her chest tightened with dread as she kept reading. "Donna was being blackmailed. She did everything she could to protect Nancy Sue. Her last entry says Leonard had taken the child to the camp. Donna went after her in a dark canyon and rescued her daughter."

"But she couldn't run fast enough. Just like Nancy Sue said," Hunter said with a sad sigh. "It's her handwriting. I remember all her notes when she was interviewing me. She had pages and pages of handwritten notes that match this writing. Much better than the fake."

The familiar sound of a gun's round clicked in the room. Marlee noticed Hunter heard it at the same moment she had. She had a split second to drop the book and grab her gun to shoot, knocking Hunter back as she put herself in the line of fire. All she knew was she couldn't let Nancy Sue lose her father.

Marlee locked eyes with Leon Carl, his gun also ready to shoot.

"Hand over the book," he demanded, his voice gravelly.

"Come and get it," Marlee said, then whistled.

But Gustav didn't come…and Leon smiled.

"They're keeping Nancy Sue company in the car. The book…for the dogs," he taunted.

Marlee's heart caught, and her stomach dropped. What had he done with Gustav and Libby? She hadn't even heard her dog bark a warning.

Neither of them.

"You're not getting anything from me," Marlee said.

"Interesting. That's exactly what your brother said when I came collecting on his debts." Leon shook his head sadly. "It's a shame what happened to him."

Stunned, Marlee could barely breathe.

Leon chuckled. "Oh, you didn't know. Yes, I was his dealer. Right up to his last fix." Leon looked at Hunter. "Imagine my surprise when my sister started dating you. She was my scout for new clients at the college parties. Then one day, she met you. And she changed. It was so disappointing. Then she convinced you to become a cop, thinking you might help her get rid of me." He laughed again, a sickening sound. "She thought she could best me with all her investigative skills she was learning in her classes. Classes that I paid for. She learned real quick with that smuggling ring you tried to take down I would always be three steps ahead of her. I told her you had to go, either from her life or from this world, her choice. She dumped you so fast. When the kid came along, I made her claim I was the father, just in case she ever got any ideas of contacting you again. I was nice about not calling in Ben's debts, though I tracked his parents for a while, just in case I changed my mind. But as long as Donna played the part as my fiancé, giving me an alias, I didn't kill you. Any of you." Leon shrugged and pointed the gun at Hunter. "That ends today."

Suddenly, Hunter ducked and kicked the book from behind Marlee across the room.

Marlee watched the journal slide across the floor, away from her and Leon. As soon as he turned his head and made a grab for it, Marlee raced forward while lifting her foot in a roundhouse kick.

In midair, she hit Leon's wrist, watching the weapon fly from his hand. But when she landed, pain from her shoulder shot through her body, sapping the last of her air from her lungs.

Marlee fell to her knees in eye-blinding agony.

As her vision cleared, she saw Leon was gone, and so was the book. An unnatural sound escaped from her lips as she cried out, but it wasn't because of her wound. Leon Carl had been her brother's dealer. Resolve to catch him sparked through her. He wouldn't get away again.

Hunter gripped the steering wheel tight, his knuckles white as he kept his eyes locked on the taillights of Leon's car up ahead. His heart pounded, a relentless drumbeat in his ears as adrenaline surged through his veins. He couldn't lose the man they were tailing—he'd stop at nothing to see Nancy Sue safe once and for all. Marlee sat beside him, her jaw clenched as she checked her weapon one more time, her injured shoulder barely slowing her down. Libby sat beside her, but Gustav was in the back of the car, ears perked and body taut, ready to spring into action the moment Marlee gave the command. Leon hadn't harmed them making his escape, but Nancy Sue had opened the car door and let the dogs out after Leon drove off with them. Hunter nearly thought the girl would jump out too, but thankfully, the rear door slammed shut on her.

He figured Leon was quite angry with the child.

His child.

"Leon's heading for the canyons," Marlee murmured, her voice tight with tension. "He's desperate. He could kill her. He doesn't care about her now that he can't use her to blackmail Donna."

"He won't get the chance," Hunter growled, his jaw set with determination. She was his flesh and blood, and he had missed out on five precious years of her life. But he wouldn't miss another minute. He was going to protect her.

Always.

The chase had been relentless since Leon snatched the diary from them. Donna's actual diary, filled with heartbreaking entries about her fears, her regrets and her desperate attempts to protect Nancy Sue. The diary was proof that Donna had known her brother was a monster, and she had tried to stop him—but she'd been too late. It was everything they needed to put Leon away forever. But none of that mattered right now. All Hunter cared about was getting his daughter back.

Leon's car swerved erratically as he neared the rocky cliffs that bordered the western edge of the park. Hunter's pulse kicked up another notch. The man was dangerous, and he didn't care who died. He'd proved that when he shot his old Army buddy to shut him up.

"Hunter, he's going for the edge," Marlee warned, her voice sharp.

Hunter surged forward, pulling up alongside Leon's vehicle. His heart lurched when he saw Nancy Sue's tiny face pressed against the back window, her tear-filled eyes wide with terror.

She sobbed, her little hands reaching toward him.

Hunter's throat went tight. "Hang on, baby," he murmured, inching ahead of Leon's vehicle. He had to cut him off before he reached the cliffs. One wrong move and that car could go over the edge, taking Nancy Sue with it.

Leon's car veered dangerously close to the cliff's edge, and with seconds to act, Hunter the car to block Leon's path, forcing the other vehicle to swerve sharply to the left. Leon's tires skidded in the loose gravel, and for one heart-stopping moment, Hunter thought the car would tip over.

But then it came to a shuddering stop, inches from the edge.

"Go!" Marlee shouted, her gun drawn as she threw open her door, taking two shots at the driver's side window, blowing a large hole in the front corner.

Hunter barely had time to put the car in Park before Gustav was a blur of fur and muscle as he leaped from the car and crashed through Leon's driver's side window. Leon's screams echoed through the canyon as the dog latched onto his arm, teeth sinking deep with a locked grip. The car jerked as Leon fought to break free, but Gustav held firm, growling low and menacing.

"Hold!" Marlee commanded, her voice cutting through the chaos.

Gustav held Leon, inches from his throat.

Hunter opened the driver's door and the man's arm.

"Off!" Marlee called Gustav off Leon, and Hunter pulled the criminal from the car, out onto the gravelly sand. He turned the crying, bloody man onto his stomach and cuffed him as he should have done six years ago. This man who had kept Donna from marrying him by threatening her child's safety and blackmailing her with the threat of death to Hunter.

"I'll take it from here. Go to Nancy Sue." Marlee put her foot onto the man's back and nodded to Hunter, indicating he should comfort the crying child.

His child.

Hunter raced to the back door, yanking it open. "Nancy Sue!"

She shied away, terror on her face, and his heart nearly broke in two.

Hunter took a deep, controlling breath and sat on the rear seat.

"I know you're scared, but you don't have to be. You helped me when I was sick, and now I want to help you."

Hunter put his hand out to her and hoped she would take it.

Slowly, Nancy Sue moved closer to him and crawled onto his lap. She buried her face in his neck and trembled with tears.

Hunter wished he could take her fear away. He wrapped his arms around her and held her tight, pressing his lips to her hair. "You're safe now. I've got you."

Leon groaned, blood dripping from his arm where Gustav had bitten him. Hunter heard Marlee calling the sheriff for backup, but Hunter could only breathe in the sweet scent of his daughter. Seeing her in such distress made Hunter want to sic Gustav on him again.

"I should have killed those dogs when I had the chance. I should have killed all of you!" Leon screamed.

"You're done," Marlee said, her voice laced with finality. "You're never hurting anyone again."

Hunter paced back and forth, calming Nancy Sue to short sniffles and felt Nancy Sue relax into only whimpers. Finally, Sheriff Hawkins and his deputies arrived, sirens blaring as they pulled up.

Marlee said, "Get him out of here." Her voice was steely. "And make sure he doesn't get another chance to escape. I want the old smuggling charges and drug-dealing charges added on. As well as murder. He killed my brother."

Hawkins nodded, his expression grim as he took Leon off their hands. He paused at Hunter by the rear door. "She okay?"

"She's going to be fine," Hunter said, his gaze flickering to Marlee. "Thanks to Marlee and Gustav, we're all going to be fine."

Marlee stepped up to Hunter and knelt by the opened door. She brushed a strand of hair out of his little girl's face. "Thank you for saving the dogs," she murmured softly. "You were so brave."

Nancy Sue reached her arms to Marlee, and at Marlee's questioning gaze to him, Hunter nodded for her to take her. The two of them had bonded at the camp, and even though he never wanted to let Nancy Sue go, the girl needed Marlee right now.

Behind Marlee, Gustav and Libby barked and ran in circles. In the next second, Nancy Sue let out a giggle.

"They're so funny." Nancy Sue stepped out of Marlee's hug to run to the dogs.

The weight of everything that had happened finally beginning to lift. Gustav and Libby circled Nancy Sue, tails wagging, proof of being proud of another day's work of tracking and protecting this little girl.

Hunter stepped out of the car and pressed his lips to Marlee's temple, his voice barely above a whisper, and for her only. "We're a family now."

Marlee smiled, her eyes shining with love. "Yes, we are. It's exactly how I dreamed it would be…minus the guns." She flashed a bright smile. "When are you going to tell her you're her dad?"

"Someday, when she's ready. But right now, I just want her to know she can trust me."

"And me too."

Marlee took his hand and led him to the child and dogs running around and playing.

As the setting sun painted the sky in shades of gold and crimson, Hunter felt something settle deep in his heart—a peace he hadn't known in years. They had rescued Nancy Sue, and in doing so, they had found their way back to each other and also rescued their future together.

Nancy Sue caught them holding hands and tilted her head. "Are you going to kiss her again?"

Marlee's sweet blush matched the color of the sunset.

"May I?" he asked Marlee, and at her nod, Hunter leaned and breathed her in, filling his senses with her perfect love.

When he pulled away, Nancy Sue's next question caught him guard.

"Is Hunter going to be an agent, too?"

Hunter shook his head, but suddenly, he wondered just how a marriage with Marlee would work. Panic raced through his heart and mind until Marlee placed her free hand on his cheek, instantly calming him.

She smiled and kept her eyes on him. "Hunter has a big,

beautiful ranch, and I'm going to train police dogs on it. There's lots of room for all kinds of puppies, don't you think, Hunter?"

His heart burst in awe. "I think you're going to change the world with your well-trained K-9s. It's perfect, Marlee."

Nancy Sue exclaimed, "I love puppies!"

Hunter smiled. "Good, because there's room for you, too, Nancy Sue. Would you like to come live with us?" Hunter held his breath as he waited for the child to choose him.

Nancy Sue lifted her head, her eyes wide and innocent. Slowly, she nodded and both he and Marlee let out collective breaths.

Marlee's eyes filled with tears. "We love you so much, Nancy Sue."

As Marlee knelt beside them, her fingers gently combing through Nancy Sue's hair, Hunter knew without a doubt that this was the moment he had been chasing his entire life. The blessing Jesus had waiting for him when the time was right.

God had opened the door, not just to Marlee, but to a family.

Hunter sent a silent prayer of thanks to God and thanks to Ben and Donna for being a part of this journey. Everything had worked out for their good. No matter how long it took them to get here.

The future was now theirs to build, and with Marlee, Nancy Sue and their loyal K-9s by their side, Hunter knew they could face anything…together.

* * * * *

Dear Reader,

Thank you for joining Marlee and Hunter on this unforgettable journey of love, redemption and second chances. Through their courage and relentless determination, they not only found Nancy Sue, but also reclaimed a future that had been stolen from them. Their path was far from easy—filled with danger, heartbreak and moments where giving up might have seemed easier. But their love, their faith and their unwavering trust in each other and God carried them through the darkest of times.

Marlee's strength and compassion showed us that even when we're wounded and weary, God gives us the courage to press on. Hunter's devotion and fierce love for his daughter reminded us that no matter how much time has been lost, God is in the business of restoring broken hearts.

Their K-9s, Gustav and Libby, were more than just loyal protectors. They were constant reminders that God places guardians in our lives—sometimes in the most unexpected forms—to keep us safe and guide us toward His will.

As Marlee and Hunter learned, God's timing is always perfect. His plan might not unfold the way we expect, but His blessings are always worth the wait. Through every danger, every setback and every heartache, God was molding Marlee and Hunter's hearts, preparing them for the beautiful gift of family and love He had waiting for them.

I love chatting with readers, and I invite you to be a part of my Novel Ideas newsletter each month. Stop by KatyLeeBooks.com to join! Hope to see you there.

Peace and blessings,
Katy Lee